Love Over Labor

ELIZA LOVEJAY

For rights and permissions, please contact elizalovejay@gmail.com

ISBN: 979-8-9923047-1-8

Chapter One

Mabel brought her fist down on the table with force. "This is *not* negotiable."

Throughout the meeting, Brick had maintained a cool demeanor, a corporate poker face, though inwardly, her gesture just now had startled him.

She continued her attack: "A living wage has to track inflation, at the very *minimum*. What you're offering is frankly insulting to the thousands of workers who make this company successful."

He answered coolly, "The company can't stay competitive if we set wages that high."

"That simply isn't true. We've done the analysis. You can make it work." She pulled a neat folder from her briefcase and held it out, locking eyes with him.

Brick accepted the folio, blinking back his surprise. He spent the next few minutes studying the documents closely, feeling the scrutiny of her gaze like a heat gun aimed at his face. She sat still and silent as a skyscraper, so the rustling of the papers cut the air, and he could even hear her *breathing* at him—a controlled breath that suggested either true and utter calm or a concentrated attempt to keep her temper. His own stress hormones were starting to spike. She had certainly done her home-work, which was going to make this even harder. It was tough to argue with these numbers, but the higher-ups had dug their heels in *deep*. He looked up and she was raising one perfectly sculpted eyebrow at him.

"This isn't realistic," Brick countered. "Your projections don't hit the mark. We have to show at least as much growth next quarter as the same period last year."

Mabel scoffed. "What do *you* consider your bottom line? The *share-holders*, your executives' year-end *bonuses*? We reject all that. You have a healthy profit margin. Obviously, we don't want to run the business into the ground because we want to keep our *jobs*."

"Crestline Industries is a corporation, Ms. McGee, not a collective. We are legally required to consider the shareholders in our nego-tiations."

"The workers are human beings, Mr. Feld, not cogs in a machine. Your shareholders don't want to *see* what a system-wide strike would do to the value of their shares. The public is sympathetic to labor in general right now, and our focus groups indicate this particular strike would hit very favorably."

"A strike isn't in anyone's interest."

"Then let's see that it doesn't *come* to that." Mabel put her hands on either side of the heavy wooden table and leaned in, bringing her face close enough to be slightly menacing. Brick noticed a freckle under her left eye, which stood out against her light brown skin like a punctuation mark. A lock of golden-brown hair slipped out of its delicate restraint and hung between them like a threat. "Dig in your pockets, and I think you'll find the spare change."

Brick didn't flinch. He was not intimidated. He was *pissed* and also a little turned on–Mabel emitted a force field that somehow both attracted and repelled him. He leaned in a little bit himself, staring into her big, brown eyes, watching her pupils dilate until he thought they would swallow him whole. He was hoping she would back down first, but the moment went on too long, and he retreated, leaning back in his chair with a sigh. "I'll bring this back to the board and see what I can do..." he urged, "...But I can't make any promises."

"You have until Wednesday." She got up and walked out without so much as a wave goodbye, swinging her hips and striking the floor rhythmically with her sensible heels.

Brick watched her go, running his hands through his dirty blond hair nervously. *Fucking hell,* he thought. *This is going to be a long weekend...*Brick had been knocking heads with Mabel McGee for several months. He was exhausted, but she wasn't showing the slightest sign of fatigue. In fact, in each successive contract negotiation meeting, she'd looked progressively fresher and *more* energetic, though he had given her little to hang her hope on. Still, he had half a mind to call her bluff. He was new to WCP Crestline Industries, and this was his first major assignment–to deal with the labor issue. He needed a win.

Chapter Two

SATURDAY

Two days later, on a Saturday afternoon, the sun was fierce, and the air humid. Brick was not exactly in the *mood* for a barbecue, but he had RSVP'd and didn't like to disappoint a friend. Anyway, getting his mind off work for a sweltering minute would be good. He needed to cool off and he needed to get out and meet people. He needed to meet *women*.

The party was at his friend's apartment complex, which had a huge community pool facility, complete with an expansive patio, decorative landscaping, and plenty of seating and shade structures. There were at least fifty people scattered about, eating, swimming, grilling, and sipping cold drinks. Sitting at a table under the shade of a large blue patio umbrella, Brick looked up from his pork ribs and nearly choked at the sight of her.

"You okay?" Rodney gave him a few hard thwaps on the back. "Do I need to do the Heimlich on you?"

He coughed violently and then took a swig of his beer. "Nah, I'm okay..." He clutched his chest, clearing his throat once more. "How do you know Mabel?"

Rodney followed Brick's gaze across the pool to where she was standing. She'd just arrived, wearing nothing but a metallic gold string bikini, a black sarong artfully wrapped into a mini skirt and a pair of bejeweled flip-flops. "Oh, Mabel? She's been my sister's best friend since forever. I've known her since we were kids. She's like *family*."

Brick raised both eyebrows. "Wow. Okay..."

"How do *you* know Mabel? Oh, wait, I know...she works for the *union*..." With this realization, Rodney flinched and put his hand on Brick's shoulder before lamenting, "...oh shit, I didn't even think about that...My bad. This is..."

"Awkward..." Brick returned. Just then, Mabel noticed him from across the patio, and they looked at each other for a moment. She gave him the slightest nod of acknowledgment and then turned back to her friend, who handed her a tropical cocktail.

"And y'all are in negotiations, right?" Rodney inquired.

"Yup. You could call it that. Nothing much is getting negotiated, though."

"She's a hard-ass." Rodney tilted his beer bottle at Brick, "Like *yourself!*"

"Yeah...with all respect, she's difficult. She's brilliant, but she's fucking *difficult*." Brick was feeling some more sensual adjectives, looking at her in that bikini, her bronze skin radiant, those long muscular legs, breasts barely contained by the triangles of her top... Damn, he couldn't go there. He looked away.

"That's her job, Brick. It's *supposed* to be adversarial."

"I get that. But we also want to get things done, and she isn't willing to compromise." He crossed his arms and looked over at her again.

"She isn't *known* for backing down on pretty much any front. But she's smart as shit, and she can figure out where the line is. She'll push you right to the edge."

"That's what I'm afraid of. Honestly, what they're asking for isn't unreasonable, but the leadership isn't interested in what's fair. It doesn't matter if I think they deserve the contract. I'm not in charge. She doesn't want to accept the constraints I'm working with."

"Hey, maybe if you get to know her socially, that will kind of grease the wheels..."

"I don't think she likes me."

"She doesn't really know you yet. She only knows you aren't giving in on the contract she wants. I'm thinking this is amazing luck y'all being at my party together."

"Yeah, maybe..."

"You should talk to her."

"I mean, I'm kind of intimidated at this point–it feels weird in this context...I mean, look at her..."

Rodney cracked up. "You mean because she's in a swimsuit? I feel you. Just keep your eyes on her face, bro. Just focus on her *eyes*. You need to keep it professional."

"*Right*. That's my point–I'm supposed to keep it professional.. In the pool.. With the golden bikini?"

"Right? But hey, keep it casual, but also not *too* casual. You know what I mean. You can do this."

"I need another drink..."

* * *

At the other end of the pool, Mabel slipped off her flip-flops, sat back on a lounge chair next to Raquel, and sipped her cocktail, stealing a glance at her current arch-nemesis.

"What is *happening*? What is *Brick Feld* doing here?"

"That fine piece of alpha male is Rodney's new friend from the gym," Raquel explained, licking her lips.

"Ew, seriously?" Mabel actually stuck out her tongue with disgust.

"Ya, he got a membership to that new gym outside town. They started working out together and getting drinks a couple months ago."

"Okay, that explains it."

"How do *you* know him?"

"He's one of the company's newest executives. I've spent *way* too many hours across the table from that man in the last few weeks."

"What? For the union? That's crazy! What a weird connection... Can you introduce me?" Raquel bolted up like she'd just won the lottery. "I've been wanting my brother to hook me up, but Rodney doesn't like to share friends...you know how he is..."

"That guy is a *jackass*."

"Come on, you know he's sexy."

"I can believe he's sexy in some *abstract* way. Maybe if I purged my memory of all the maneuvers he's pulled, I would be able to perceive that streak of handsome, all those..." she looked over at him, standing shirtless, talking to Rodney, "... abs."

"That's right! Ooo, girl, I want to run my hand over that man's chest...How do you not *see* all that?" Raquel was fanning herself dramatically now for effect.

"All I can *see* is his ego and his ambition. He's classic upper management—a pathetic *bootlicker* on the one hand, but also a heartless *pig* whose only passion is climbing the corporate ladder."

"That's harsh."

"No, seriously, Raquel, he's a bad person! Don't try to date him. I'm surprised Rodney is even hanging out with him. I thought your brother had better taste!"

"My brother doesn't hang out with assholes. He must see something you don't, Mabel. Ugh, you are always so *sure* of yourself..."

"That's because I'm so rarely *wrong* about people."

"No one's perfect, not even you..."

"I am not perfect, I *admit* that. But he's a clod, he's a blunt instrument, like his *name*! What kind of a name is *Brick*? It makes me think of stone, like *cold as a stone*, or *hard-headed*, or dumb as a *rock*..."

Raquel had picked up her phone now and was typing into the search bar. She looked up and smirked at her friend. "It's an *English* name, Mabel, and it means 'good guy' or 'mason.'"

"Well, that's ironic. He's an asshole."

"Whether he's an asshole or not, I think you should work this connection—maybe Rodney has some inside information that could help you, some psychological warfare kind of material."

"Now I *like* where you're going with that idea."

"Also, playing nice might be a thing."

"Nah."

Raquel just sighed.

* * *

Mabel's laughter was staccato and melodious, like a flamenco guitar refrain. Brick had never seen her smile, much less laugh, and it transformed her face from pretty to *beautiful.* Her hair was down, and he was surprised at how long, thick, and wavy it was. At their meetings, she always wore it back in a neat bun, either at the nape of her long neck, or perched on the top of her head. She appeared to be holding court, surrounded by six or seven other people, and telling a story about some mishap she'd had at the grocery store. Her audience was rapt and intermittently cracking up.

Brick walked over and sat on the edge of the pool to listen, hanging his legs down in the water, nursing another beer. He saw Mabel seeing him–her eyes followed his movement for a moment–but she didn't acknowledge him, and it *irked* him. He was used to getting female attention, and the other women in the pool *definitely* took notice. He smiled at them and nodded his head, but he suddenly wanted *her* attention, and rather desperately. She was wet, and her caramel skin glistened in the late afternoon sun. He *tried* not to look, but her nipples pressed against the gold bikini top, daring him to imagine, against all propriety. His dick was getting hard, and this affected his judgment even more than the 7.9% microbrew. He got a wild, very immature impulse and could not contain the urge. When she had finished the story, and there was a lull in the conversation, he splashed her vigorously. She looked up, blinking her eyes, and he smirked.

"What's up, Mabel?" he asked.

A chorus of "Oh!"s and "Oooo!"s from Mabel's friends forced her to engage. She paused for a beat, pondering the move. The next second, she retaliated with disproportionate force–a splashback that he could only interpret as a ruthless deterrent. She was not *playing,* apparently. He nodded. That checked out. He only *slightly* regretted the gesture.

"Watch it, Feld." She didn't smile but met his gaze with the intensity he was accustomed to.

He held up his hands and smiled with mischief in his eyes. "Truce."

"For now." She raised both eyebrows at him.

"For now." He nodded, making his face serious again.

Brick set his beer on the edge of the pool and dropped into the water, dunking his head under and bobbing back up to standing. He was smiling at her now, a sheepish look on his face. In negotiations, he always kept a stone face, but now even his eyes were smiling, and she hardly recognized him. It was a little unnerving. As he moved toward her, Mabel noticed the way the beads of water stuck to some parts of his chest and rolled down other parts. She felt an animal desire well up inside her and resented her body for its betrayal–Raquel was right; there was no denying he was a hottie. His dirty blond hair had changed to dark brown and was now slicked back, wet against his head. This revealed a very slight receding hairline. Damn straight, he wasn't *perfect*. Ha!

"Weird coincidence, right? Us being at this party together?" he asked her. She could see he was trying to act casual. Mabel caught him stealing a glance at her chest, and she popped it out a bit because maybe she could work this angle to her advantage regarding the contract negotiations. She didn't mind toying with him, at any rate.

"Yup, pretty unexpected," she replied, relenting and giving him the slightest suggestion of a smile.

"So...you know *Rodney*?" he inquired.

"Yes, we go *way* back. He's like a brother to me. I heard you two work out?"

"We met at the gym, yes."

"I'm not *surprised*." She nodded knowingly.

"You mean you're not surprised I work out?" He smiled broadly now, flexed his arms a little, and ran his hand through his hair. She was sure he had seen the way she'd eyed him just now.

What a peacock! She shook her head at him. "No." Now Brick looked offended, which made Mabel laugh out loud. She raised one eyebrow, "Well, true, I'm not surprised you *sculpt* yourself..." She stopped short of calling him Adonis, though he qualified. "But what I *mean* is, I can't think of any other way you and Rodney could become friends."

He tilted his head. "What are you trying to *say*?"

"Rodney is just a down-to-earth, genuine, *community-minded* guy. He is a high school teacher and a poet. *You*, on the other hand, are a corporate executive. Usually, oil and water don't mix."

"Ouch!" Brick flinched theatrically. "Ok, so I work at a corporation.

You put me in a box, Mabel. You don't know me. I am more than my job. I think you would be *surprised*..." He folded his arms across his chest in protest.

"If you want to *really* surprise me, you can sign the contract." She folded her arms across her own chest, and her cleavage erupted. She could not help but notice that *he* could not help but notice her luscious curve. *Ha! I've got him*, she thought, smiling devilishly.

"That's not fair." He shook his head at her disapprovingly.

She shrugged at him and put her hands on her hips. "Actually, that's exactly fair. Prove me wrong about you and sign the *contract*."

"Mabel, seriously, the contract is not just about *me*. I think you know that. I am personally sympathetic to your demands–I mean to the *workers'* demands. I've been thinking about it nonstop–it's keeping me up at night."

Mabel noticed a *maybe* authentic look of concern on his face. Or *maybe* he was just gaming her. "If you really care, come to the table ready to negotiate," she erupted.

"I *do* want to negotiate. How about we meet up on our own, ahead of the next meeting, just to look more closely at it?" He raised one eyebrow at her with the question.

"Another meeting before Wednesday?"

"Not an official meeting, just a palaver over dinner. I think the corporate office is a little formal, a little like a pressure cooker. I can speak more freely if it's off the record and over a bottle of wine."

She stared at him for a long time, trying to discern his intentions. He met her gaze and kept still, awaiting her answer. She narrowed her eyes–*palaver*? Now, she was thrown off balance because that word didn't fit her idea of who this man was. And what was his game? Was he trying to hit on her, or was he serious about working out a compromise on the contract? Either way, she supposed it would be strategic to take him up on this dinner idea. She suddenly dunked down, giving into the heat and getting her wild mane of hair wet, staying submerged a good ten seconds to consider the prospect of an unsanctioned meetup. When she popped up, Brick was looking at her with a bit hungry wolf eyes, taking in the look of her wet hair, which was darker now and hanging much longer down her back.

"Okay," she agreed, "But we should meet in the city. This town is too small—we can't be seen together. Meet me at The Heights downtown at 6 P.M. tomorrow night."

"I'll be there!"

Chapter Three

SUNDAY

Mabel had to nail this meeting. She stood in front of the mirror, debating what to wear. Chris, who was the union's second negotiator, was coming along to this dinner because she needed a witness. He was encouraging her to use all of her feminine 'potential,' as he put it, to get the best contract possible. It was part of the game, he said. Mabel wasn't opposed to this strategy, and she had seen the way Brick looked at her in the pool yesterday. It would be silly not to take advantage of his attraction, but she wanted to maintain professionalism at the same time. It would have to be subtle. She had a reputation to uphold. She chose a sleeveless blouse with a slightly more open neckline. Rather than wearing her hair in a bun, as she usually did for work, she artfully braided her long, wavy locks into a thick plait that hung low over her right shoulder. Her long, layered bangs still framed her face. She added sparkling earrings and a darker shade of lipstick and smiled knowingly at her reflection.

Mabel arrived early, as always. She entered the restaurant and noticed it was a lot dimmer than she remembered. Looking around, she saw the place was packed, mostly with couples having intimate candle-light dinners. There was a buzz of quiet conversation layered over jazz music and servers busily criss-crossing the floor carrying trays of food and drinks. Here was a couple leaning in to talk, their faces a mere inch or two apart. There was another, entwining their fingers across the table. Next to *them*, two young lovers sat sipping suggestively from wine glasses, playing footsie under the table. This wasn't exactly the vibe she was going for. She approached the podium to check in. The host smiled at her.

"Hi, I'm Mabel McGee. I have a table for three?" Mabel choked back a guffaw at the inadvertent rhyme. Her laughter was contagious, and the hostess chuckled, too, looking down at her roster. She looked up and grinned, chiming in, "Mabel McGee, follow me!"

Mabel considered being a dork and following up with *another* rhyme, but just then, her phone buzzed. She looked down. It was Chris, texting her that he was running late. Ugh. Typical. Now she would have to greet Brick *alone.*

The young woman led Mabel to a lovely, secluded table at the back of the seating area.

"You know, I hate to be annoying, but do you have anything in a brighter, busier location?" Mabel asked, desperately looking around the restaurant.

"Um...ok...let me see..." She ran her eyes down the list and scanned the room. "It looks like we're full tonight for the dinner hour. I'm sorry."

"No worries. Could I start with a whisky and coke?"

"You got it."

It was a square table, and Mabel selected the power position, sitting with her back to the wall. At the center of the table sat an ornate bud vase displaying fresh flowers and a short glass centerpiece with a flickering candle. She picked up a menu and skimmed the entrees. Her mind veered to the last time she'd had a romantic dinner. It was more than six months ago, that third date with Colin, whom she'd met through a dating app. Unfortunately, Colin ended up being a real piece of...

"Your second is here, along with the whisky and coke."

Mabel looked up to see the host holding forth her drink with one hand while simultaneously using the other hand to present Brick with a small flourish.

"Thank you," Mabel said, smiling at the host and accepting the drink. She turned to Brick, who was dressed a little more casually than she was used to seeing him at the office. He had on a brown tweed dress coat and a blue button-down shirt but no tie. His clothes fit him just right, accentuating his broad chest. *Oh great*, she thought, *he's playing the same game...He knows he's cute. But he doesn't know I think he's cute... do I really think he's cute?*

"Good evening, Mabel." He did a strangely formal bow, then looked up and smiled broadly, a genuine warmth spreading across his face, and put his hand out. All this was a bit unsettling, but Mabel set the drink down and stood up to shake his hand, making eye contact with her own sly smile. She was confident that she could work with this chemistry and still remain professional. Brick had a firm handshake, one she'd experienced and reciprocated on numerous occasions, but this time, she held his hand a little longer and gave an extra squeeze. She nodded with the squeeze as she said, "Brick."

He sat down across from her and said, "Thank you for coming tonight."

"Of course," Mabel replied.

"Can I get you a drink?" asked the hostess.

"Could I get a gin and tonic, please?" Brick asked.

"Certainly."

"Thank you." Brick turned back to Mabel and glanced at the place sitting next to her. "Are you expecting someone else?" he asked.

"Yes. I invited Chris. I thought it would be wise to have another person here."

"Ok. That's...fine, I guess." Brick couldn't help but feel disappointed. He wanted to focus on convincing *one* person–the most important person for this negotiation. God dammit, now he was sure they would double-team him. One layer beneath the worry about the contract, Brick was disappointed because he had been a *little* excited to just hang out with Mabel alone. Not like this was a date or anything, but she kind of fascinated him, and she was quite beautiful tonight, a long, thick braid slinking across her shoulder, grazing her bare collarbone, looking all sparkly and sipping a cocktail. He noticed he was sweating and shook his hands out a little under the table.

"We're still keeping this off the record, right?" he confirmed.

"Yes, that's my intention. Just our little secret." She smiled coyly and sipped from her drink, enjoying the sweet, sharp bubbles that mirrored her demeanor.

"That's why you picked this secluded spot, right? You're strategic at every turn, Mabel. I respect that."

Mabel tilted her head and then nodded. "Yes, well, it pays to think ahead."

"So, while we're waiting for Chris...tell me about yourself. You grew up here, right? You and Rodney?"

"That's right. I have strong ties to this community. I have all my family here, a big extended family, and I have friends that go way back."

"That's cool. I miss that."

"You're from out of town, right?"

"I'm very far from home. I grew up around San Francisco," Brick answered.

"You left that mild climate in a major metropolis for all *this*? Was it worth it?"

Brick smiled. "Is the *job* worth it? The humidity is killing me, but I mean, the salary is *amazing* ..."

Mabel raised her eyebrows at him. "So you moved away from your friends and family for the six figures?"

"Yeah, but money isn't *everything*. I like the money, but I also need to feel at home, like I can fit in. I've only been here six months, so I'm still getting the feel for the job, the town... Rodney's been taking me out a little."

"Stick with Rodney. He's good people."

Brick nodded. "For sure. Rodney's great. What do you like to do for fun around here?"

"Karaoke, bowling, rock climbing..."

"Seriously? I've always wanted to try that!"

"Which one?"

"Rock climbing!"

"There's lots of crazy climbing spots in the west. I'm surprised you've never done it."

"I always wanted to. I just never got a chance when I was a kid–it's expensive, and I didn't grow up like that. We didn't have money for sports equipment or extracurriculars." Brick shrugged.

"Really?" Mabel asked, raising her eyebrows at him, " I guess I just assumed you were upper class, born and bred."

"Nope," Brick asserted, shaking his head. "I know most people in my position are like that, but that's not me."

"You definitely act like it at the office."

"Well, when you're one of the rare bootstrappers, you have to adapt and kind of blend in with the culture around these companies." Brick noted Mabel's skeptical expression and added, "I mean, I'm aware I'm a white guy, so it's easier for me than for a lot of people..."

"Yup. I've never been able to 'blend in'. I have no experience with that. Is it weird to be almost undercover? I think I would have a hard time faking it all day."

"It's frustrating. They just want everyone to conform. I can play the game, but I don't relate to these people who have never struggled a day in their life."

"Well, I'm sorry I judged you, but you put on a good act!" Mabel shrugged. "Anyway, I don't come from money either, so you're in good company. You can let down your hair with me."

Brick smiled, feeling his guard dropping dangerously low. "Thanks, Mabel."

She nodded. "But getting back to rock climbing, now that you've infiltrated, you've *got* the extra *money*..." she asked him, "What's stopping you from getting out there?"

"I think I just need a mentor."

"It's not Jedi training," Mabel teased. "You can take a *class*, you know."

Brick chuckled. "Yeah, I can do that. I'd rather learn one-on-one."

"Private lessons, then," Mabel stated.

"Are you offering to show me the *way*?" Brick raised one eyebrow, and one corner of his mouth indicated a playful confidence, a projection of his boyish optimism.

"Me? Oh, I'm not an instructor. I think you want someone bonded, you know, with insurance."

"I don't need insurance because I *trust* you, Mabel."

"Really? *Why?*" Mabel asked, eyeing him suspiciously. He was talking out his ass now, just trying to flatter her.

"I'm good at reading people. You have integrity. You're smart, you're responsible. You're clearly athletic..." He couldn't help looking pointedly at her smooth, toned, and muscular upper arms. Mabel noticed him looking and drew her index finger down her bicep very slowly. *God dammit!* Brick loved an athletic woman. He imagined not just rock climbing with her but running, biking, working out at the gym, working out in the bed...he mentally slapped himself *hard*. This was not a date, not a date! Mabel was off limits.

"I'm guessing you're *at least* as competent at climbing as you are at negotiations." Brick continued, thinking that strength and strategy were part of both skill sets.

"I've been climbing a long time, I know my way around a rock wall. And safety is *always* my number one priority."

"See, I knew it! When can we start?" Brick sat up and leaned in, looking like a puppy.

"Patience, Padawan," Mabel teased, holding both hands up in protest. "I'm glad you find me trustworthy, considering the situation. Trust is important in this relationship. I mean, workplace, you know... But...I think we need to keep this...professional. Fraternization is frowned upon, as I'm sure you know. We could both get in trouble just for having this dinner."

His face fell. "Yeah, conflict of interest and all that. You're completely right." He shook his head. "It's too bad because I think under other circumstances, you and I could be friends, Mabel."

Mabel smiled in earnest, helplessly revealing a tickle of thrill at that notion. Ugh. This man felt like a needle slipping under her skin. Truthfully, she liked the idea of teaching him to climb. She had a feeling Brick would be a quick study and competitive in a fun way. "In another timeline, maybe...Where's Chris? It's not like him to be late like this..." She looked down at her phone nervously. She was anxious to get down to business before Brick said anything else warm and fuzzy. This man was the enemy, and she had to keep that fact at the top of her brain. She didn't like to stand in muddy waters.

Just then, a server came up to the table, a pretty young woman wearing her dark hair in a long ponytail.

"Hi, I'm Janine. I'll be your server tonight. What can I get you two love birds?"

"Oh, we're not–" Now Mabel was blushing.

"No, that's not what this is. It's just a work meeting," Brick interrupted.

"Oh, my bad. Well, business friends, what looks good?" Janine corrected quickly, her own cheeks beginning to flush.

Brick hadn't even glanced at the menu yet. He'd been so focused on Mabel's face, her words, her voice. Now he saw her blush, and it was so endearing–it was a whole other side of her he couldn't have imagined until that moment. He picked up the menu and scanned for a moment, zeroing in on a safe bet. "I'll have the chicken parmesan, please. And... could you bring us a bottle of your best pinot noir?"

"Of course." She nodded, then looked up at Mabel.

"And...I'll have the Florentine, please."

"Great! Thanks, guys."

Mabel and Brick both chimed in, "Thank you," at the same time, then looked at each other, smiling awkwardly. Janine took the menus and sauntered off to the next task. Brick watched her go and Mabel watched him watching her. Then her phone buzzed, and she picked it up.

"Oh, noooo!" Mabel burst out.

"What's wrong?" Brick asked. By the way her face looked, he wondered if someone had died.

"Chris isn't going to make it...he's got a family emergency. Dammit." She put her hand on her head and grimaced.

At that moment, Brick felt a guilty wave of relief wash over him like a cool breeze. *Now* he could get something accomplished...and get to know Mabel a little better in the meantime. "That's too bad..." he said, feigning disappointment. "But we can still discuss the contract, right?" he asked her.

"I guess so.." Mabel looked up at his big, hazel eyes and felt the flower of a forbidden crush beginning to bloom someplace deep inside. She suddenly regretted this whole escapade. What was she thinking?

This shit was highly inappropriate. Time to get to business and then get the *hell* out of here. She reached down into her handbag and pulled out a small notebook and a pen.

"Let's do this," she declared.

"Ok, let's get started," Brick agreed and leaned in.

"We will *not* negotiate the wage demands. Period. Don't even try your charm on me, Mr. Feld."

Mabel could see Brick was taken aback. She had surprised even herself with that little comment. He nodded, withholding a smile. "Ok. I don't think the company will go for it, but I will do my best. What about maternity leave? Six months is not going to fly."

Mabel shook her head. "Women need to be able to stay home with their babies. They need the bonding time. They need the recovery time."

Brick reached out and touched her left hand, which was holding the notebook. "Mabel, I hear you. I think there may be a compromise there." Mabel tried to look unaffected, but her stomach was a whirlwind of butterflies. Why was the merest touch of his hand doing this to her? She was very disappointed in herself. He continued looking deep into her eyes, his hand still lightly resting on hers. She was helpless to look away. This moment was going on for too long, and Mabel felt she was slipping into a hypnotic trance. She had to break free!

"What's your offer?" she finally blurted.

"I'll ask for five months, but I'm guessing they won't do more than four."

"Five is an absolute minimum." She used this moment as an excuse to pull her hand from his and held up the five fingers as a warning. She narrowed her eyes with the gesture.

He pulled his hand back. "Okay, okay, I'll do my best."

"What about the break times?"

"That should be doable."

"Benefits package?"

"We can meet you halfway."

"Oh, so I can get half of a cataract surgery?"

"You can't demand the salary increase *and* better benefits in the same cycle."

"I sure can."

"I recommend you wait for the next contract to bump benefits packages. I'm just being real, Mabel."

"Again, I should wait until the next cycle to be able to afford a life-saving procedure? You know you have employees who won't go to the E.R. when they should because the copay is too high?"

"Jesus, I get it. It's fucked up," Brick exclaimed, shaking his head. He wished he hadn't cussed just now—it made him seem unprofessional, ineloquent. He was letting his guard down because he wanted to get close to this woman, and it was hard to hide it now. "I'll do what I can, Mabel. Like I said, some increase in benefits is possible, but they aren't going to go for that number."

"We'll see."

Just then, the bottle of wine arrived. "Business is taken care of to the highest extent possible," he proclaimed. "May I pour you some wine?"

Against her better judgment, Mabel smiled and held out her glass.

Chapter Four

MONDAY

"I thought you said he was a jackass." Raquel looked up at Mabel, who was about a quarter of the way up the rock wall. She took up the slack as Mabel climbed higher and higher, expertly choosing the holds.

Mabel waited till she got her foot on a larger wedge-shaped hold about halfway up, and took a break. She looked down at her friend and tried to explain: "Well, I might have judged him too harshly at first. We had dinner the other night and–

"What? You went *out* with him?" Raquel's eyes were fit to fall out of her head, and the pitch of her voice shot up an octave.

"Whoa, relax. Don't drop me, okay? No, I didn't *go out* with him. It was just a work meeting. He wanted to meet off the record to see if we could make progress on the contract. I'm climbing on."

Raquel shouted, "Climb on," up to indicate she was giving slack and continued to belay Mabel up the route, ready to catch her if she blew the crux. "Um...I think he's into you. I saw him looking at your chest in the pool." Raquel had to pull up the rope frantically to keep up with Mabel, who was now nearly to the top of her project, a 12b that very few people attempted due to the technical difficulty.

"Well…" she sighed, breathing heavier with the effort, "that's just every straight man in the presence of literally *any* woman."

"Nah—I mean, *yes*, I get you, *men,* but I was watching him, and I saw how he was looking at *you,* not *just* your tits."

This gave Mabel pause. In the pool, she had the feeling he was attracted to her, and at the work dinner, she started to think he was a little *into* her, as a person. This was not a thread she wanted to pull on, although the thought of it sent a tingle down her spine. When she got to the top, Mabel looked down and gave the thumbs-up signal that she was going to rappel down. Raquel loosened her grip on the rope and let it skim through her hands until Mabel touched down in front of her, putting her hands on her hips and picking up the conversation.

"I mean, yes, I noticed it, too, and I leaned into that." Mabel smiled devilishly at her friend.

"You are so scandalous! You told me not to date him, and then you flirted with him!?"

"I know, I know—I wasn't really trying to hit on him. It was more like dangling bait. It was just a strategic thing. I was working the string bikini to get the *contract*…"

"Right. You keep telling yourself that." Raquel nodded knowingly at her friend.

Mabel hit her on the arm playfully. "No, but actually, at the work dinner, I saw another side of him and…I can't believe I'm admitting this to you, but all day, I keep thinking about him in an inappropriate way, in a *non-work* way…"

"You mean his beautiful body? Girl, I told you!"

"Yes, it *is* the body, and his irritatingly flawless skin, and his big, hazel eyes. But it's not just the looks. He has this confident, super masculine persona that is still kind of *sweet* somehow…I don't know. It's hard to explain."

"What happened to your *values,* Mabel? You must be coming off that high horse cuz I thought you hated corporate tools…"

"He's not as much of a corporate tool as I thought. He's not a rich boy, surprisingly."

"He's an exec. He's making a lot more money than you and me. I personally wouldn't mind that in a boyfriend, but…"

"But he grew up different. He didn't come from money. He was raised by a single mom. He's the oldest of three, and he supports his siblings–one has a drug problem, and—"

"Dang, you got personal, Mabel. I thought this was a *work meeting*?!"

"It *was* a work meeting. And that's the other thing–he was so sincere about wanting to help us get the best possible contract..."

"All of a sudden, he wants to get you a good *contract*, now?"

"Well, I pressed him, and he's going to try again with his boss, so he says. I don't know, I mean, he could be stringing me along."

"No. You got under his skin."

"No, no, I mean, he was friendly; he likes me, but it's not like *that*." Mabel looked away when she said this, a classic tell that Raquel noted.

"Did he offer to pay for dinner?"

"Yes, but I didn't let him. It wasn't appropriate for him to pay for anything for me, obviously. I think he was just being nice."

"He likes you, Mabel! He was hitting on you!"

"He didn't *hit on me*, and I'm glad he didn't because that would be inappropriate. He was totally professional. But I got a good vibe, you know?"

"So what you're saying is that you were *wrong* about him?"

"Yes, I'm admitting I was a little bit wrong about him, okay?"

"And you like him now?"

"He said he thought we could be friends, and I think that's true. Under *other circumstances*, I think he and I would get along. He actually asked me to teach him to climb..."

"Oh shit, yes! Let's take him climbing at Mocanaqua!"

"I can't, Raquel, come on. I can't introduce a conflict of interest. That would *not* go over well with the union."

Raquel sighed. "Well, *I* could take him..."

The thought of this actually made Mabel jealous, but she didn't say so. "Only if you can get past Rodney!" she taunted.

Raquel just rolled her eyes.

Chapter Five

TUESDAY

At seven in the morning, the sun was just creeping up over the horizon. Mabel wasn't used to getting up quite this early, and she felt groggy and a little sore from the workout last night. Still, the longer she walked, the more her mood expanded because the light regime was so beautiful, and she couldn't remember hearing so much birdsong ever in her life! She had her coffee in one hand and gripped a long dog leash in the other. Fifi was an elegant Afghan hound with very long, luscious, honey-colored fur and pedigree posture. Fifi was happy to stroll casually for the first half of the walk but picked up the pace as they drew nearer to the dog park, pulling the leash taut in a delicate effort to speed Mabel along.

When they turned the corner, their destination was in sight, and it was already hopping with canines, some sniffing each other warily, some engaged in playful sparring, some chasing tennis balls. Fifi barked her greeting from across the street, and all canine eyes and ears pointed in her direction for a moment. Several dogs abandoned what they'd been involved in and ran to the fence, jumping and barking wildly. *I guess Fifi is popular!* Mabel thought. When they entered the gate, Mabel released

Fifi into the fray, walked over to the bench on the opposite side of the park, and sat down to enjoy her coffee.

She scanned the motley collection of doggy parents scattered in small groups, adding their chatter to the morning bird chorus. At the far end of the park, under a sycamore tree, Mabel spotted a tall figure whose shape and swagger she recognized immediately and which set her heart to pounding–it was almost audible–and she blushed. There was Brick, talking with an older woman who reminded Mabel of her own grandmother. The woman was wearing an old-fashioned red and white flowered scarf tied around her head and a lightweight yellow cardigan, and she was peering up at Brick with a knowing smile. Mabel couldn't make out what they were saying, but she caught the timber of his voice, and it sent a tingle down her spine. She watched him like he was a nature documentary, studying his every gesture. From the body language, she could tell he had some rapport with the old woman. Mabel just couldn't stop staring and was considering whether she should say hello or try to sneak out when he must have felt her eyes on him because he looked pointedly up and in her direction, and she saw his face light up, and he waved at her. She waved back helplessly, smiling, then took a swig of coffee.

Now she was stuck. *God dammit.* She watched him turn back to the woman and continue the conversation. She was surprised–disappointed?--that he hadn't immediately come over to say hello. She noted her own feelings–*was she really crushing on this man*? Mabel was beyond bruised from her last breakup and actively worked to counter any romantic tendencies in herself right now. Her focus was work and family, health and happiness. No man required, no man desired. She comforted herself with the thought that any relationship with Brick was out of the realm of possibility–completely forbidden. *Look, but don't touch.*

A few more minutes passed, and she thought maybe she should just gather Fifi and go, but then she saw Brick say goodbye to the old woman, touching her lightly on the arm. The old woman waved at him warmly, and he turned and strode over to where Mabel was sitting. She decided to stay seated and tried to look casual, though the closer he came, the faster she felt her pulse.

"Good morning, Ms. McGee," he beamed, standing in front of Mabel, nodding his head at her with a smirk.

"Good morning, Mr. Feld." She smiled at him and shook her head back and forth. "Twice in a week we happen to run into each other, huh? Are you stalking me?"

"Nah, I think *you're* the stalker because I've never seen you at this dog park, and I come here every morning. Do you live in the neighborhood, or is this some weird union *espionage*?"

Mabel chuckled. "No, that kind of work is above my pay grade."

Brick cocked his head at her. "Sure. That's just what a spy would say..."

Mabel laughed again. "I thought you *trusted* me?!"

"So did I..." he returned, raising an eyebrow at her.

Mabel put both hands up. "I'm just dog-sitting for a friend who lives in this neighborhood," she confessed, "Fifi is my friend's dog." She gestured at Fifi, who was in the middle of a play bow with a handsome chocolate-brown Pitbull with a white belly.

"Oh, I know Fifi! Hey, girl!" He walked over and greeted her, leaning over and putting his hand out. Fifi sniffed his hand, gracefully licked his face, then went back to her play.

"Really?" Mabel was flat, incredulous.

"Yeah, she's a regular. That pit bull is *my* dog," He gestured to the very dog Fifi was engaged with. "That's Roswell."

"Oh really? He's cute...they seem to get along *well*..." Just now, Fifi was sniffing at Roswell's butt, and he was wagging his tail in her face.

Brick chuckled. "Yeah, they play a lot. It's hilarious. Fifi is so fancy, but she really cuts loose with him-"

Mabel laughed, watching Fifi tower over Roswell as he playfully nipped at her leg.

After a beat, Brick walked back to the bench and sat down next to Mabel, leaving a respectable distance between them. He watched her take another sip of her coffee and couldn't help noticing the way her full lips wrapped around the opening of the travel mug. She was without makeup and looked lovely, her skin glowing in the morning sunshine, her cheeks flushed. He tried not to stare and carefully avoided looking at the scoop neck of her tank top.

"And...so...you know *Chaundra*?" Mabel asked. She felt her skin getting hot now and hoped she wasn't visibly red. Ugh.

"Yes, actually, Chaundra is one of the first people I met at the dog park when I moved here."

"Okay...interesting." This was a small city, but still–how did Brick happen to know *two* of her close friends? Mabel shook her head. "She's never mentioned you."

"I mean, I know her just from the dog park–she's a casual acquaintance. It's not like we're close friends or anything. We mainly talk about our dogs. And our annoying bosses."

"Oh, so you know about Mr. Hendrick Pfeiffer?"

"The freaky fashionista with a sadistic streak?"

"He's so crazy. I don't know how she can stand to work at that office."

"Yeah, he makes my boss look tame."

"I wouldn't go that far. Pfeiffer provides everyone with a respectable salary and great benefits."

"How does that work? I know Crestline Industries is a subsidiary of WCP, so why are things so different over *here*?"

"Pfeiffer is the sole owner of the WCP corporation, but he doesn't really mess with any of the subsidiaries–he lets them manage their own business, literally. He's very generous when it comes to profit sharing with his direct employees in the parent office. They've never organized a union over there because the working conditions are so good."

"What about those required 'retreats' where you have to do highly inappropriate things in the name of 'team building'?" Brick asked, raising an eyebrow.

"Okay, yes. They definitely need to unionize to deal with *that* nonsense. Do they even have an HR department? What the hell?"

"I know, right? How's your boss?"

"Oh, she's *amazing*. Andrea has been involved in union work for forty years–she's seen it *all*. She totally supports me. She's more like a mentor than a boss."

"That must be nice. You know, I've never had a boss I've actually liked."

"What? Are you saying you *don't* like Stewart Lowe?" Mabel bugged her eyes out, teasing him.

"He's pretty much a garden variety CEO. He's not the *worst* person I've ever worked for..."

"*That's* really scary, Brick." Mabel shook her head.

"That's the corporate world." Brick shrugged.

"You made your bed, and that's where you gotta sleep." Mabel shrugged back. She suddenly felt awkward, as if referencing a bed was a tell or something–like a Freudian slip. It was getting hard to sort out how much of this feeling was just a game she was playing and how much she actually desired him.

"Yup. But I'm not sleeping too well right now." He wasn't sleeping well, literally, because of the stress of this contract *and* because he couldn't stop thinking about Mabel. She was so off-limits, but she was so enticing. He'd even dreamt of her last night–in the dream, he was in the pool with her again, and she was in that gold bikini...When he'd spied her from across the dog park, his nervous system had exploded, sending blood to all the wrong places. He had a lot of practice controlling his behavior, so outwardly, he appeared very calm and collected.

"Not making any headway with our contract?" Mabel asked, steering the conversation away from beds.

"Well, Mr. Lowe was out of the office yesterday, but–"

"Let me guess, he likes to take a pretty regular three-day weekend?" Mabel asked, rolling her eyes.

"He's usually out two Mondays per month."

Mabel shook her head. "It must be nice..."

"I'll find a way to persuade him. You've got us with the numbers. I just have to put the right spin on it."

"Or the right pressure. I'm very serious about a strike, Brick." With this, her face changed to stone, and all trace of warmth and congeniality vaporized in an instant.

"Oh, I know. I've got this."

"You're very confident. I hope that's warranted."

"Trust me. I have a plan."

"Okay. I hope it's a good one. Hey, I better go..." Mabel uttered quickly, looking at her watch, and stood up, gathering the leash from the bench. "Nice to see you, and good luck with your boss."

Brick stood up and nodded. "Thanks. Nice to see you." He watched her call Fifi and attach the leash. She turned and waved once more before strolling to the gate. Brick watched her and felt a sharp pain in his chest.

* * *

By the time he'd prepared his arguments, it was almost 2 p.m. Brick stood up from his desk and stretched, shaking his arms out and rolling his shoulders. He took off his jacket and got down to do twenty-five pushups just to pump his blood and his confidence and ease the anxiety. Then he took five deep breaths, put his coat back on, and chugged the last of his afternoon coffee. He took the elevator up to the top floor, walked down the hallway, and approached Lola's desk, feeling the dread return like a swarm of gnats.

"Hi, Lola, how's it going?"

Lola looked up from her computer monitor and smiled broadly at Brick. She was dressed in her usual designer silk blouse and fitted trousers. She flipped her long black hair over her shoulder with a sassy swish. "Oh, I'm okay. How about you? Are you okay? Your color is a little off or something..."

"I'm...no, I'm good, yeah, I'm not *bad*...is Mr. Lowe available?"

Lola looked skeptical. "He's definitely back from lunch. Let me see if he's busy." She picked up the phone and dialed his extension. "Hello. Mr. Feld is here and would like to speak with you..." There was a long pause, and Brick could hear the tiny animated voice of his boss coming from the receiver, the suggestion of words that he couldn't quite discern. "Okay, sir." She hung up the phone and rolled her eyes. "He'll see you. Go ahead in."

"What's the weather like in there today?" Brick gestured with his thumb at the big mahogany door, looking very concerned.

"Something's brewing with him today–cloudy with a chance of a thunderstorm, I'd say. I hope you brought your *rain gear!*"

"Oh shit." He felt his shoulders tense.

"Don't shoot the meteorologist." Lola put her hands up, smiling.

He laughed nervously. "How could I shoot you? I rely on your intel, Lola. Thank you." He started toward his boss' office.

"Good luck in there!" Lola cheered.

"Thanks..." Brick twisted the doorknob and pushed through, disappearing into the abyss.

"Good afternoon, Mr. Lowe," he began.

"Hello, Mr. Feld. What brings you in?" Stewart Lowe poured himself a glass of something light brown and highly alcoholic. He gestured toward Brick with the ornate bottle, raising his eyebrows in a silent question.

"No, thank you, sir. I want to discuss the contract with the union."

He sat back down at his desk with his drink and invited Brick to sit across from him. "Excellent. How's that going? Are we settled?"

"No. That's why I'm here. They are pretty determined to win on a few key points."

Mr. Lowe laughed. "They're about to hit a *Brick* wall, am I right?"

Now Brick laughed nervously. "Well, yes, I suppose, but I suggest we build a door in that wall because they're threatening to strike."

"They're bluffing."

"I don't think so, sir."

"Trust me. I know these people."

"You've worked with Ms. McGee before?"

"I've met her. Spunky young thing. I bet *she's* a nice piece of ass."

Brick was offended on her behalf and also desperate not to give the slightest hint that he was, indeed, attracted to her. "She's a *pain* in the ass, actually." Mr. Lowe smirked. "But," Brick continued, "she has the workers behind her."

"You're new to this. You aren't used to bringing the intimidation factor. You've got to feel your power. You've got to believe you will conquer. They can smell fear, Feld." Mr. Lowe was making a fist with his right hand, holding it up like a prizefighter. He looked ridiculous, and Brick was sure this man had never been in a fistfight.

"Oh, I'm not afraid of her," Brick replied, keeping his voice calm and confident. "However, I *am* concerned about the optics of a strike.

I've run the numbers, and for about a 15% reduction in profits, we can bump the salaries, extend maternity leave–"

"No! Absolutely not!" Mr. Lowe stood up from his chair, nostrils flaring. "I offered them a bone, and they threw it in my face like spoiled brats. We can't let them push us because the next time they come to the table, it'll only be *worse*. They'll want *more*."

"Profits are up. We can make some concessions and stay in the green, but if we go into a strike, depending on how long it goes on, that could make a bigger dent than the new contract."

"This is all nothing but a tantrum, and we don't negotiate with God damned terrorists! I didn't get to be CEO by sharing profits with the workers, Mr. Feld. That's not my job. And it's not *your* job. *Your* job is to secure the best deal for the corporation, for the shareholders."

"Yes, of course." Brick tugged at his collar, feeling a tightness in his throat. "Are we prepared to wait them out if they *do* go on strike?"

"We've never had a strike at this company. I'm telling you, they're bluffing."

"But if they aren't?"

"We starve them out. Make that bitch realize that we *will* starve them out, and she *will* think twice about a strike. I'm putting that on you, Mr. Feld. You need to scare the shit out of her."

Brick sat shaking his head, inwardly seething, groping for the words that would both put this asshole in his place and let him keep his job– but did he really want to keep this job?

"You're right out of 1995, Mr. Lowe. Haven't you heard we don't call them bitches anymore?"

"What? Oh, you're funny, I get it. But you know what I mean, Feld."

"Yes. I understand. I'll get back to you when we have an agreement." Brick stood up and moved to walk out of the room.

Brick walked out feeling sick to his stomach. He was going to have to find a way around Stuart Lowe.

Chapter Six

(Text messages)
Brick: Hey Rodney. Can I get Mabel's cell from you?
Rodney: Um...I don't know about that, bro.
Brick: It's a work matter. Nothing shady. I need to communicate with her off the record.
Rodney: Okay, let me check. I'ma add Raquel

* * *

Rodney: Brick wants Mabel's cell. Should I give it to him?
Raquel: You trying to set them up?
Rodney: Nope
Raquel: Something's going *on* with them!
Rodney: It's not what you think---
Raquel: Did you see them in the pool on Saturday?
Brick: Hi Raquel, it's Brick. It's just work. I need to talk to her about the contract.
Raquel: Oh, whoops...I didn't know you were on this. Wow, my bad,

ignore me, I was running my mouth. I know y'all had a work meeting recently.

Brick: Sorry if I caught you off guard. I'm trying to contact her about the contract negotiation, that's all.

Raquel: Of course, that makes sense…

Rodney: So we're good to share contact?

Raquel: All good

* * *

Brick: Mabel, this is Brick. I got your number from Rodney.

Mabel: WTF…Okay…Where were you today? I thought we were working together on this.

Brick: I called in sick!

Mabel: Are you actually sick, or are you a fucking coward?

Brick: No, I'm not sick. I told them I had the stomach flu to stall the meeting.

Mabel: You didn't stall the meeting! They sent Marshall!

Brick: Wait WHAT?

Mabel: He's such a dick!

Brick: Oh no…that was not the plan.

Mabel: You seriously thought they would wait for you to get better?

Brick: Yes!

Mabel: Damn, you are green.

Brick: I needed more time to convince the board.

Mabel: You fucked over the union, you fucked yourself, and you fucked the company.

Brick: Fuck.

Mabel: We're going on strike tomorrow.

Brick: Oh no.

Mabel: Oh yes. Kiss your year-end bonus goodbye.

Brick: That's not the point.

Mabel: For us, it is.

Brick: I'm with you, Mabel.

Mabel: Nah, you are management all the way. I thought you were different somehow.

Brick: I AM different.
Mabel: You are ALL the same. Enjoy your sick leave. Corporate gets all
the time they need, am I right?
Brick: Well, yes...

That was the last he heard from her. He texted a few more times, but she
didn't respond, so he gave up. *Shit.*

Chapter Seven

THURSDAY

Throngs would be an understatement. It looked like half the city was out in the streets today. Looking down the boulevard, Brick couldn't see the end of the crowd in either direction. It was a sea of signs, and people were singing and chanting. Mabel certainly knew how to mobilize! Brick had expected nothing less, which was why he'd wanted to avoid all this. Still, it was kind of beautiful from this perspective, from the ground, inside this crowd of voices uniting. The early morning sunshine sent highlights through everyone's hair, and their signs were glowing like stained glass. At the moment, it was still cool enough to be comfortably mashed up against people. Brick saw a whole lot of passionate baby faces chanting along with the union members. The college students were out in full force! Classes at the university hadn't started up yet, but by mid-August everyone was back in town and still had a lot of time on their hands.

Apparently, an all-call had gone out because, based on the signs and T-shirts he could read from where he was standing, there were people from the nurses' union, the teachers' union, and service workers international out supporting the strike. It was easy to identify his company's employees, as they all had their matching red union shirts on. The biggest cluster was in front of the corporate office. Scanning the crowd, he spotted Mabel standing at the bottom of the stairs going up to the plaza, talking to Chris, who was working the welcome table, along with a few other members who were busy greeting people, serving coffee, and handing out signs. Mabel was in her red union T-shirt, and her hair was pulled back in a ponytail. She was gesturing wildly, and Chris had a concerned look on his face.

Brick started to weave his way through the crowd but got stuck behind a drum line, which gave him the opportunity to admire a truly exquisite hand-made sign that said, "An Injury to One is an Injury to ALL." Suddenly he felt a hand on his shoulder and turned around to see Rodney, wearing his teacher's union T-shirt, of course.

"Hey, man, what's up? I thought I'd see you up on that top floor looking down. It's refreshing to see executives participating in the strike!"

"Hey, Rodney! Yeah, I'm not *officially* participating...I just came to see Mabel, actually."

"Business or pleasure? It looks like the *business* didn't work out." Rodney assumed, shrugging.

"I fucked up. This wasn't supposed to happen." Brick shook his head.

"You knew Mabel was serious though."

"Deadly serious. So serious, I'm afraid she hates me now."

"Are you *into* her?" Rodney cocked his head with the question and raised an eyebrow.

"Can I tell you about it later? I really need to talk to her." Brick had a look of desperation in his eyes, and his voice conveyed urgency.

"For sure," Rodney reassured, "Good luck with that." He watched Brick pick his way around the drummers and disappear into the maze of people. Then he texted his sister.

* * *

Brick walked up to the information booth, running his hand through his hair. Chris spotted him first and hit Mabel on the shoulder. "Oh my God, it's Brick Feld!" he gasped, his eyes bulging.

"What?" Mabel looked up and jumped out of her skin. Brick was practically incognito, dressed in a T-shirt and jeans, hair disheveled. However, he still had his signature confident, golden-boy posture, apparently shameless, even in the face of all this.

"Hey, y'all. Can I get some coffee?" He smiled nervously at Chris first before turning his gaze to the object of his desire. Her hair was in a long ponytail sticking out the back of her union baseball cap, and her union T-shirt hugged her curves.

"What are you doing here? I thought you were *sick*." Mable's eyes were poison darts, and Brick actually felt a piercing sensation in his heart.

"I came to apologize for my naivete–I made a strategic error, Mabel."

"Yeah, that's an understatement." She folded her arms and Brick could swear there was smoke coming from her nostrils.

"Stuart Lowe is a despicable person," Brick spat.

"You *just* realized this?" Mabel scoffed.

"It has really crystallized...I met with him on Tuesday and tried to bring him toward a middle ground, but he doesn't want to concede anything. He didn't believe you would actually strike."

"He's fucking delusional!" Mabel cursed, shaking her head.

Brick nodded. "He's a lot of things–stubborn, arrogant, selfish, sexist..."

"Your boss is a textbook psychopath," Chris fumed, breaking into the conversation. He also reached out to Brick with a cup of steaming coffee, like a peace offering.

Brick nodded his agreement. "Thanks, Chris." He took a sip and turned back to Mabel. "That's why I was planning to talk with the board because I know a few of the board members are definitely more rational, and maybe more sympathetic to the workers..."

"It would be hard to be less sympathetic," Mabel retorted, rolling her eyes.

"Are you here to support the strike?" Chris asked. From his body language, he had the distinct impression that this man was *really* here to try and get in Mabel's pants. What surprised him was that he could also see that Mabel was fighting some kind of romantic urge herself. She was watching Brick intensely, waiting for his response.

"Yes, I am. I can't imagine being up *there* right now." Brick looked up to the top floor, where Mr. Lowe no doubt stood, staring out the window, fuming. "Things feel different from down here. I think more executives need to get out of the office and actually immerse themselves in the real work of this corporation. It's too easy to forget about the people who make these profits possible."

"Amen! We have a convert!" Chris grinned and put his hand up to Mabel in a gesture that communicated, 'Good job, you worked your magic!' She smiled at Chris, accepting the praise, but left him hanging. Her arms were still folded over her chest, and she wasn't ready to give in, to believe. Mabel raised one eyebrow at Brick. She was only inching toward a place of trust again with this man.

Brick was noticeably uncomfortable, and Mabel decided to just keep staring at him silently, content to watch him squirm. Their eye contact went on a little too long. However, right at the end, she betrayed her internal struggle—a flicker of warmth passed between them, and she blinked it back, letting out an exasperated sigh.

"Thanks for the coffee. I'm going to walk around a little," Brick said, putting a hand up to wave goodbye.

"Mmhmm. Go 'head." she answered, practically shooing him away.

* * *

"Hey, Rodney! Thanks for coming out!" Mabel gave him a bear hug. "God, I love the teachers' union..."

"Right? We gotta represent."

"I appreciate you. You know we will definitely return the favor."

He nodded, but then his face changed from a warm smile to a look of concern. "What's up with you and Brick?" he queried.

"What do you mean? You can see what's *up*..." She gestured around at the crowd. "He blew us off."

"Yeah, but now he's here instead of up in his office."

"Yup, and he's a damn fool. I don't know what he's doing down here...actually, I do know, he's *trying* to play both sides–"

"He's playing at *you*."

"I don't know what you're talking about."

"Mabel, come on now. You ain't stupid."

"What? What are you talking about?" She was blushing now, feeling suddenly exposed and deeply conflicted.

"He's into you."

"Did he tell you that?"

"I can see it. Why else is he down here, risking getting fired?"

"He says he cares about the workers and supports the strike."

"No doubt."

"He doesn't actually care." Mabel shook her head and rolled her eyes.

"I think he does. But that's not the reason he's here." With this, Rodney stared her down, seeing right through her defensive ploy.

"Ugh. Why are you even friends with him?" Mabel sighed. "Why do you care about some random guy you met at the gym?"

Rodney shook his head. "I didn't meet him at the gym, Mabel. I *recognized* him at the gym. I had seen him around at work because he volunteers in the learning center twice a week after school. He's a volunteer math tutor."

"Oh..." Her face softened, and her eyes went wide. Mabel's mental projection of Brick shifted yet again. He was beginning to contain the multitudes.

"He really connects with the students, and he's a good math tutor. And he comes from a working-class background, Mabel. He's more like us than you think."

"I know, I know. And I know he's putting his brother through college, and he's paying for his sister's drug treatment and all that."

"You over here tryin' to act like you don't like him..."

"I'm doing my job. I like him, okay, but he's my enemy, Rodney."

"Is he?"

* * *

Mabel's speech was ad-libbed, but she was nothing less than eloquent, poetic, even! Brick was standing in the front row, just a few feet from the stage, holding up a sign, utterly captivated. She spoke with the cadence of a natural-born rabble-rouser, hitting all the high notes: love, labor, loyalty, and, of course, a living wage. With each pronouncement, the crowd swelled, erupting with applause, cheers, whoops and hollers. The collective spirit was raised by her words, and the ferocity of her voice, and the people felt their power. They believed in their cause, and they believed in the certainty of their triumph. Brick, too, was swayed and felt a lightness come over him. At this moment, he realized he wasn't meant to be a corporate executive. There was something more he wanted from his work, from his life. And there was something more he wanted from Mabel McGee.

When she finished her speech, the applause went on for literal *minutes*. She smiled, waved to the crowd, and handed the mic to the next speaker. Then she pressed her palms together, making a gesture of gratitude to all who had shown up today. She descended the stairs stage left, and Brick quickly weaved his way over there to greet her.

Her face was flushed, and she was sweating from the exertion and the heat, but she looked more beautiful than ever, and Brick nearly swooned. He caught up to her and touched her arm gently to get her attention. She stopped and turned to find him wide-eyed.

"Hey, you're still here!" she teased. "And you got a sign! Traitorous! I like it!"

"Mabel, wow, what a speech!"

"Thank you, Brick," she beamed. "You're very kind."

"I knew you had a way with words, but that was something else. It was sublime, I mean, it was incredible how you worked the crowd. You created a tidal *wave*!"

Mabel was flattered by this statement and also a bit alarmed. He was speaking so fast and he actually looked *nervous* now. Maybe Rodney was right. Maybe he was actually really into her... She was really feeling her own power after that speech, and now this...

"I'm just doing my job..." Mabel shrugged, "Wait till you hear Yessica speak!" She smiled at him, and his eyes grew yet another degree wider.

"Hey, do you want to sit down in the shade over there?" he asked, pointing to the cluster of trees across the lawn.

Hope made his face luminous. Of course, he was also shiny with perspiration. *It can't hurt to sit and talk with him for a minute,* Mabel thought. She became aware of walls coming down inside of her, crumbling suddenly as if a tremor was all it took to undermine the structural integrity of her resistance. *Either that, or I'm about to collapse with heat stroke.* She looked at him and cocked her head. "Um.. sure, I could use a break. It's so hot!" she observed and fanned herself with her hand.

Walking side by side, they skirted around the edge of the crowd, heading toward a cluster of trees at the corner of the plaza. Brick spotted Sam, the town ice cream guy, pushing his tiny refrigerator cart along the edge of the lawn.

"What's your favorite flavor?" Brick asked her, pointing at the cart.

"Mango," Mabel announced without hesitation.

"Nice. I'll meet you in the shade," he said. Mabel nodded and watched him run over to the truck. He was so graceful and so muscular, and somehow, he was able to exert himself, despite the considerable heat of the day. It was all she could do to keep walking, desperate for some shade. She saw him greet Sam, slapping hands with him like they were old friends, and pull out his wallet and buy two popsicles. By the time he got over to the trees, Mabel was sitting on the grass. She was cooling off, in a sense. On the one hand, at least the surface of her skin was cooler, but on the other hand, internally, she felt her body getting hotter the closer he got to her. He handed her the mango popsicle and sat down beside her.

"Thank you! This is perfect!" She took off the plastic wrapper and plunged the popsicle into her mouth, savoring the icy sensation, wanting to cool it all down. Brick watched her, and she saw him in her peripheral vision and turned to look at him, her mouth full. She had the distinct feeling that he was wishing *he* was that cold, sweet popsicle. He pulled off the wrapper of his own frozen treat and bit off the tip.

"What's that? Orange cream?" she asked.

"Yup," he nodded.

She licked around the bottom of her popsicle because it was dripping, and the thing was too big to fit entirely into her mouth. Brick proceeded to nurse his own popsicle, never taking his eyes off her. Despite her valiant efforts, sticky orange fluid was running down her hand. Brick imagined licking the juice from her skin. Somehow, he, too, was feeling hotter here under the tree despite the shade and the cold popsicle on his tongue.

"Aren't you worried about being seen here?" Mabel asked when she'd reduced the popsicle to a more manageable size and had time to come up for air. "You're supposed to be sick, and you're supposed to be on the other side of this whole thing."

"I'm not tied to this job, Mabel. If they fire me, whatever. If they don't come to their senses soon, I'm probably going to quit anyway."

"You moved across the country for this job."

"Yes, but...I realized this week that it's not for me. I can't work for someone like Stuart Lowe in the long term."

"I hear you there."

"Also, Mabel..." Brick paused, looking at her, just letting the orange cream drip down his hand. "I don't want to be in this position where.. where I can't be your friend."

She withdrew the popsicle from her mouth. "Oh." She was blushing now, again, and she felt his gaze on her, and it was blazing hot.

"So, you want to be my friend badly enough to lose your job?" she asked.

"I want it that badly."

This statement hung between them for a moment.

"If we're going to be friends..." Mabel suggested, "Can I taste your orange cream?"

"Sure..." He held his popsicle out to her, and she put her mouth over the tip and sucked on it, looking into his eyes. His heart was racing now.

"Thank you. It's delicious. Do you want a taste of mine?"

"Yes, please..."

She reciprocated, holding forth the dregs of her bright orange mess. He licked it up the side, and she gasped, dropping the popsicle and leaning toward him. He saw it in her eyes and dropped his own popsicle into the grass, reaching for her. She turned her body, rolling onto her knees to meet his embrace. Mabel's sticky hands grasped his face and looked into his eyes, then their mouths merged in sweet surrender. He could taste both popsicle flavors on her lips. She could feel his tongue was still cold, but only for a moment. He kissed her into oblivion until the heat of the day and the heat of her body were indistinguishable, until the sounds of the crowd, now roaring again, faded far away, and only her heartbeat kept time. This eternal kiss caught the eye of a local journalist who was out covering the strike. She snapped a photo with her massive camera, framing their faces with the union sign behind them, which Brick had leaned up against the tree. They took no notice.

Chapter Eight

FRIDAY

Mabel's legs were very strong, so why did she feel all jiggly? Sure, she'd started her morning run a little preoccupied– strategies around managing the strike swirled with memories of Brick's mouth: the sweet, sticky warmth of his tongue, the way his hands felt on her waist...Ug... She kept trying to push the moment out of her mind and get back into her leg muscles and her rhythmic breathing, but it seemed like at every damned corner, it slapped her in the face. She'd never noticed before how very *peppered* the town was with those dang newspaper boxes! Wasn't physical print supposed to be in decline? The front page of the local newspaper featured her forbidden kiss prominently, with the headline "Love Over Labor? Strike continues!" She blushed deeper each time she saw the picture until her cheeks were practically ablaze. Everyone else was over at the rally. The crowd was going wild...Why was that reporter skulking around at the far corner of the park at the exact moment she'd lost her mind and kissed Brick Feld in broad daylight?

Instead of the usual euphoria she got from the physical exertion of running, she felt exhausted, anxious, and ashamed. Plus, her phone was tucked into the right sleeve pocket of her leggings and buzzed relentlessly throughout the run, tickling her thigh and adding to the sensory and emotional overload. She sprinted the last block and then slowed to a walk, panting, shaking her arms out as if expelling demons. She avoided making eye contact with people passing her on the street and walked to the park to use the water fountain. Twenty long sips later, she sat down on a bench and pulled out her phone to check the damage.

* * *

Mom: Why didn't you tell me you were dating someone new? I had to find out from the *newspaper*?
Mabel: We're not dating.
Mom: That's not what it looks like to me.
Mabel: It's not what you think. I'll come over later and explain, okay?
Mom: Your father is very concerned.
Mabel: Please tell him not to worry!

* * *

Charlotte: Mom is mad at you for hiding your affair from her.
Mabel: It's not an affair! We aren't dating! He works for the company!
Did any of you actually read the article?
Charlotte: Skimmed it...I mean, there is speculation in the article about you having an affair.
Mabel: They just want to sell papers! You actually think I would jeopardize my work that way?
Charlotte: The kiss looks pretty hot. You're gonna have a hard time denying it.
Mabel: Well, I'm going to deny it because it isn't a thing.
Charlotte: Wait, are you about to get fired?
Mabel: I hope not.
Charlotte: Shit.
Mabel: Don't tell Mom!

* * *

Chris: Um...I saw the paper...Was this part of your plan?

Mabel: No! What kind of plan would that be?

Chris: I can see how seducing Brick would be useful. You shouldn't have kissed him in public, is all I'm saying. He's useless to us if he's fired.

Mabel: I wasn't seducing him! I just fucked up. I'm so embarrassed! Andrea has been calling me, and I can't bring myself to answer.

Chris: Play it off as a publicity stunt? More people are reading about the strike now, right?

Mabel: I don't think she'll believe me. Anyway, I don't want to lie to her.

Chris: Don't lie. Just play up the positives!

* * *

Raquel: OMG Mabel! The KISS...I feel like I'm in a romance novel! Are you freaking out?

Mabel: I'm freaking the fuck out!

Raquel: I knew you were really into him. I told you he wasn't an asshole!

Mabel: It doesn't matter. I can't do this.

Raquel: You're the protagonist. You will come out on top. You will find love, and you will triumph at work.

Mabel: This isn't a romance novel, Raquel! And it's not about me. I need to do what's best for the union, what will win them the best contract. I was selfish to indulge in that kiss!

Raquel: No! You were just caught up in the moment. It's not your fault.

Mabel: It's totally my fault.

Raquel: I'm your best friend. I know what to say to calm you down. Just take a breath. It's all going to work out.

Mabel: I don't know how...everything's fucked.

* * *

Rodney: So...when I was talking Brick up yesterday, I didn't think you would go and do all that...

Mabel: Yes, I partially blame you for the kiss, Rodney.

Rodney: You could have waited until the negotiations were over.

Mabel: Thanks, that's helpful.
Rodney: Sorry. Let me know what I can do.
Mabel: Please just keep Brick out of my hair. He keeps calling. I can't deal with him right now.
Rodney: I'll try...

* * *

Andrea: We need to talk about the kiss. Come see me when you get into the office, please.
Mabel: Will do.

* * *

Chaundra: I didn't realize you knew Brick!? He's one of my dog park friends! Are you going to get in trouble for this? Call me! I want to trade stories!
Mabel: It's so weird you know him... Everything about this is so weird.
Chaundra: You think that's weird–I will tell you some crazy stuff from this last work trip...
Mabel: Can't wait to commiserate! I'll call you later. I have to deal with my boss...
Chaundra: Good luck!

* * *

Brick: Please answer the phone. I need to talk to you.

* * *

"What the hell is *this*?" Stewart Lowe held up the newspaper with the photograph. Brick flinched.

"Sir, let me explain," Brick cautioned, holding up one hand and breathing slowly to keep his cool.

"You weren't sick on Wednesday, were you?" Mr. Lowe accused.

"Not exactly..."

"God damn, Feld, you're pussy-whipped."

"First of all, that's offensive."

"It's fucking accurate!"

Brick shook his head and sighed. "Second of all, we aren't sleeping together. It was one kiss in a moment of weakness, but Mabel has nothing to do with this."

"My ass! Loyalty, Feld. This company is about loyalty. You betrayed me. She used you. She used her feminine witchcraft on you. God dammit, Feld, you wanted to get in her pants, so you stalled the meeting!"

"No! I stalled because Mabel simply convinced me, with rational arguments and sound math, that we needed to make some concessions! I admit I've come to like her as a person, but that is separate from how I do my job. The stall wasn't her fault. It wasn't like she was coming on to me *at* all."

"That's not what it looks like here!" Stewart Lowe held up the newspaper *again*.

"It was my fault. I apologize for the public display of affection. Of course, public or not, it was inappropriate for me to kiss her while we were still working together. I acknowledge that."

"She played you, Feld. I'm surprised you fell into the trap. You let your *dick* do the thinking. I was young once. I can relate." He smiled a smarmy smile that nauseated Brick.

"Please STOP. It's not what you think at all," Brick fumed, standing up with such force that it knocked his chair over backward, and the chair made a huge thud sound on the floor behind him. "I was trying to find a compromise that would be in the best interest of the company. I tried to tell *you* they were going to strike, and you didn't believe me. I was buying time on Wednesday, and you sent in Marshall."

"*You* are responsible for the strike. *You* gave them the idea they had a chance. If I'd sent Marshall in from the start, we would not be in this position."

Brick thought about this for a moment–he had to consider the possibility that he had warped the union's response. Would Mabel have caved in that scenario? If Marshall had been there from the beginning? "No. You're wrong," he said sternly. "In the past, maybe, but these are different times. Working people are pushed to the edge, and they are going to jump. They have no choice. You and the board and the rest of the execs, you don't get *it*."

"*You* don't get it. Your job is dangling from a string. Get it together, Feld, or you're fired."

Brick stood up and walked out without another word. He left the chair stranded on its back.

* * *

Andrea held the newspaper aloft and pointed at the photo.

"This really doesn't look good, Mabel," she uttered, shaking her head.

Mabel flinched at the expression on her boss' face. "I'm so sorry..." she sighed.

"The union negotiator *literally* in bed with the company...."

"No. I promise you, Andrea, we aren't sleeping together. We never slept together. It was just that one kiss."

"I know you. I know you wouldn't betray the employees. But people are talking, and they are *very* upset."

"They have every right to be upset. I was totally unprofessional, so out of line–"

"What were you thinking, Mabel?

"I wasn't thinking at all. I'm pretty sure I was suffering from heat sickness–I was delirious. I'm not excusing myself from responsibility, but you know it was over 100 degrees yesterday?"

"I know—climate change. But a kiss like that doesn't materialize out of thin air–or even thick, humid air. There's something you aren't telling me. This is just so out of character... What's really going on with you two? I thought you despised him?"

Mabel dropped her head to her chest and closed her eyes for a moment. Andrea watched her in silence.

Finally, Mabel lifted her head and looked at her boss. "So I ran into him last weekend at my friend's barbecue," she confessed, "and he wanted to meet up over dinner, off the record, to discuss the contract."

"You didn't, though." Andrea raised her eyebrows, making her statement seem more like a question.

"I did..."

Andrea put her hands to her forehead. She was frankly shocked at her protege. "Have I taught you nothing?"

"It seemed like a good idea at the time..." Mabel continued, blushing furiously.

"Was he coming on to you?" Now, Andrea looked angry in a protective way.

"No. No, not at all. He was very professional. I think my guard was down a little, and I found that he's actually a pretty nice guy...by the end of our conversation, he seemed to honestly want to push on the CEO and the board to get the best deal possible for the workers."

"But then he didn't show up at the *actual* meeting. He let Marshall take over."

"I thought the same thing initially. I thought he *must* have been playing me, but then he came down to the strike yesterday, and he said he had called in sick because he was stalling–he thought they would just postpone the meeting another day or two, and he was planning to go directly to the board–"

"You told me for months he was an immovable object, and now he's suddenly switched sides? If that's the case, you can't believe this has nothing to do with you personally, Mabel."

"I mean...yes, he obviously *likes* me..." Mabel's expression and tone of voice betrayed her. She was sure Andrea could see that she had feelings for the man. "But I think I also convinced him to look at the facts, the numbers, and work for what's fair."

"Either he's fallen in love with you, like a crazy love that he's willing to lose his job over, or he's a double agent, and his goal all along was to manipulate you, to make you think it was going our way."

"I don't think he would do that, Andrea."

"Your judgment is impaired. You need to step away from this contract."

"Andrea, please–"

Mabel's expression could only be described as guilty-puppy-dog.

Tears started to stream down her face. Andrea leaned in and put her hand on Mabel's shoulder, softening her voice.

"You need to take some time off and reflect on your decisions and how you got here. This isn't a termination, Mabel. It's just a strategic move. The union values you, it needs you, but right now, it needs you to back off."

Mabel wiped her eyes. "Okay. I'd still like to support the strike."

"Mabel, take today off, lay low this weekend, and let this whole thing cool down. Yessica can hold down the strike."

"But—"

"I'll call a general membership meeting for next week, and we'll decide on the next steps. Just be patient."

"Okay. I'm just...I'm so mad at myself."

"Be kind to yourself and unflinchingly honest at the same time. You made a mistake, that's all. You need to analyze that." Mabel nodded.

"Thank you, Andrea." She stood up and walked around the desk and they had a nice long hug.

"Of course. Hey, on the bright side, we now have the press and the public very interested in this contract! You couldn't have planned a better publicity stunt."

Mabel laughed into Andrea's shoulder. "Okay, but still, I want to kill that journalist!"

* * *

Esteemed board of directors,

I would first like to apologize for my unprofessional behavior at the strike. I violated a basic law of workplace relations and jeopardized the reputation of the company and the union. It was honestly a moment of weakness I can't fully explain, but you have my word that, up until that moment in the park, which was unfortunately captured in time for perpetuity, my relationship with Ms. McGee had been one hundred percent professional and platonic. What brought me to that moment also brings me to this moment.

I'm writing to tender my resignation from this corporation. While I've learned a lot this past year, I can no longer continue to work under the leadership of Mr. Stewart Lowe. He has a management style that stifles open communication, creativity, and collaboration across departments. His vision for this corporation doesn't include the welfare and well-being of the rank-and-file employees who make this company what it is. The profit margin can't be the only thing that matters if you want to have an ethical and sustainable business model. This company can do better, but it won't as long as Mr. Lowe is CEO.

I called in sick on Wednesday because, on Tuesday, I was unable to convince Mr. Lowe to make even the smallest concession despite my warning that the workers would certainly strike. I thought that by staying home that day, I could buy time and avoid the strike. My plan was to come to the board and see if you would listen to reason. Mr. Lowe did not believe a strike was imminent, and sent Mr. Robert Marshall into the meeting that day, knowing he would bulldoze any attempts at further negotiation. This was a strategic error so great, it could be almost criminal.

I've attached my recommendations for the contract, along with calculations and projections showing we can afford to make these changes. Much of this work was done by Mabel McGee. I checked the math and built on it. I've also attached transcripts from some interviews I conducted informally while I was circulating among the workers at the strike on Thursday. They gave me permission to share their stories with you, as well as the reporter who put us on the front page. I hope you will see that these people deserve a good contract and that the company can absolutely afford to give it to them.

Thank you for your time.
Sincerely,
Brick Feld

Chapter Nine

SATURDAY

Raquel entered the bar and spotted Mabel at the far back table. She was dressed like she just rolled out of bed. Her hair was a damn mess, and her slumped posture reminded Raquel of fresh roadkill. Raquel watched her friend sip her cocktail lethargically through a tiny straw and thought she hadn't seen Mabel this fucked up since she'd broken her ankle in 11th grade and had to miss the rest of the soccer season. She walked up behind her and whacked her on the shoulder. "You look *terrible*!" she scolded.

Mabel looked up, dragging her eyelids, then her neck, and finally her torso until she sat upright enough to glare at Raquel as she sat down across from her. "That's because I feel fucking terrible!"

"But you can't go out like this. Snap out of it!"

"It's your fault. You asked me to come here! And anyway, it's good I look like shit! Hopefully, no one will recognize me. I don't want to talk to anyone."

"My God, at least put your hair up." She pulled a hair tie off her wrist and handed it to Mabel.

"Thanks," Mabel mumbled, accepting the offering. Then she scraped her mass of disheveled hair together and wound it into a giant bun, fully exposing her sullen face. She was truly almost unrecognizable in this state. Mabel McGee looking anything less than perfectly put together was a *very* bad sign.

"Did you sleep at all last night?" Raquel asked.

Mabel shrugged. "A little," she uttered nonchalantly.

"I brought you a few things." Raquel lifted her oversized leather handbag onto the table and pulled out a small tin of gummies. "For your sleep," she ordered and pushed it across the table.

"Thank you. I'll try that," Mabel surrendered, picking up the tin and reading the label.

"To distract you from your troubles..." Raquel pulled out the newest novel by Mabel's favorite author. Mabel's face brightened, and a small smile flashed across her face.

"You're the best, Raquel!" she gushed. "I need this!" Mabel snatched the book, held it to her chest, then turned it over to read the back.

"And..." Raquel said, "Here." She pulled out a long white envelope with Mabel's name written on it in black ink. She gingerly slid it across the table like she was poking a piece of raw meat through the bars of a cage.

"What's this?" Mabel looked up from the novel, brows furrowed.

"It's from Brick."

"Oh no..." Mabel shoved it back across the table. It nearly careened off the corner and onto the floor if not for Raquel's lightning reflexes.

Raquel glared at her now. "What? Are you serious? He gave it to Rodney to give to me to give to you because you won't answer texts, calls, emails..."

"I'm not touching that," Mabel swore, shaking her head.

"Mabel, you have to talk to him."

"No."

"At least read the letter, Mabel. Or just tell him you aren't interested."

"No, it's not that...it's not that I'm not interested..."

"So you *are* interested!?"

"I like him. I told you I like him! But this is all a mess, and I'm feeling flooded like I'm actually underwater. I don't know what I want because I can't breathe."

"Just keep the letter and read it when you're ready. He's not going anywhere, trust me." With this, Raquel pushed the envelope back again.

Mabel stared at it for a minute, then sighed, picked it up, and put it in her purse. "Fine. I'll keep it. For now."

"Thank you! Damn, you're difficult! Now let's talk about your strategy—what are you gonna say at the union meeting?"

Chapter Ten

MONDAY

Mabel was back to looking like Mabel again, even if on the inside she was still a mess. Her hair was pinned up in a neat bun and her makeup was cleverly applied: so natural it was barely noticeable. Considering the scandal, she definitely wasn't going for sexy tonight. The slightly tinted lip gloss, light mascara, and dewy moisturizer gave her a wholesome look and made her face pop and glow. She wore a modest red blouse, signaling her loyalty to the union.

From her seat on the stage, Mabel watched the room fill up to the very brim, with people standing at the back, lining the wall. The ceiling fans were going full blast, but it was still too hot to be comfortable. She took a deep breath in through her nose, and let it out through her mouth. Chris, Andrea, and a few other union officers were sitting next to her for moral support. She looked at her watch and then at Andrea.

"Are you ready?" she asked, raising her eyebrows at Mabel.

Mabel nodded, rolling her shoulders back and checking her posture, steeling herself and feeling her body tensing with the effort. "Ready as I can be!" she answered, flexing her feet, working to counter the nervous energy with a wave of calm awareness of her muscles.

"You got this," Chris encouraged, putting a hand on her shoulder.

Human touch always helped. Mabel turned and smiled at him. "Thanks!" she expressed and stood up, smoothing her slacks. She walked over to the podium and tapped the mic. It was definitely on. The chatter in the room diminished as she looked around and made eye contact with as many members as she could.

"Brothers, sisters, siblings, good evening, everyone," she started, "Thank you for letting me speak tonight. First, I am here to apologize for my behavior on the first day of the strike. I'd like to blame it on the heat, and it was definitely hot that day, no pun intended..." Here people chuckled, and a few sucked their teeth.

"What are you doing with your mouth on that asshole? He's a corporate dog," somebody shouted.

"You needed to keep it in your pants!" came a voice from the back of the room.

"Come on now, Harold, you are jumping to conclusions," Andrea rebuked, shaking her head.

"I kissed him one time, that's it, that's all," Mabel admitted, and then she watched a couple of young women in the front row look at each other and roll their eyes.

"Mmhmm. You're a traitor," criticized the one on the left

"You're a traitor! I don't care if you didn't literally sleep with him. You slept with him!" accused the one on the right.

"I know what it looks like. I know what it seems like," Mabel acknowledged. "I know what they've been saying in the paper. Don't believe everything you read, friends. Do you think she called me before writing up all that piece of speculative fiction? We are not sleeping together. I never slept with that man." Mabel wagged her finger and shook her head, a look of disdain on her face. "But I'll tell you what, that article got a lot of attention on this strike, a lot of eyes on our cause," Mabel continued. "Our strike is now making national news! And that article got one thing right: Brick and I *were* actually working together."

"Working for who? For what? He's on the other side. They always are!" came a young woman's voice from the front left.

Mabel located the woman and made eye contact with her. "It's true he was not working with us at first," she admitted, "but in more recent meetings with Mr. Feld, I had come to believe he'd had a change of heart."

"He didn't give us a contract! How is that working *with us*?" the young woman snapped.

"He told me he was going to push for many of our demands despite the barriers on his end. He actually called in sick last week to try and stall the negotiations—"

"So you're playing *games* now? You know I'm not getting paid this week, right? *You* all are still getting paid," she ranted as she pointed at Mabel and the other union officers, "but we are broke! Am I right?" People were nodding, and their faces conveyed frustration, anger, and despair.

"Listen, please, listen to me." Mabel put up her hands. A hush spread unevenly across the group. Mabel waited. When it was utterly silent, she continued. "I understand you are upset. You have a right to be upset. But I need you to believe me when I say that I never betrayed you. I'm named after my great-grandma, Mabel Collins. She left Alabama almost a hundred years ago now, okay? She left the Jim Crow South to come North for something better. How many of y'all have family who migrated from somewhere else to come here to find a better life?" Mabel scanned the audience, noting that roughly a third of the crowd had raised their hands. She nodded her head, acknowledging their struggle.

"So, you know what I'm talking about!" Mabel continued. "My great grandma came to Pittsburg with my uncle and auntie, and they all got jobs in the steel industry, you know? It was so much better than Alabama, so much better!" People were clapping and whooping. Mabel put up one hand, her index finger pointed to the ceiling. "But that didn't mean the working conditions were great. Nah. Bosses are bosses, North or South." People were nodding and affirming that statement. Mabel let it ride a moment and then picked up again. "Good thing my family was able to join the union! My family joined the United Steel Workers in the 1920s, y'all! My family has *always* been Union." The group cheered in agreement. Mabel put her fist in the air. "I was raised to believe that we *all* deserve a life of dignity, we all deserve to have a living wage and a fair share of the fruits of our own labor!"

Just then, the heavy double doors to the meeting room opened, and Brick Feld walked fervently in and straight up the center aisle, holding forth a thick stack of paper in one hand like a torch at the Olympics. He was dressed in his office garb and seemed to be on official company business. All heads turned, and a collective gasp was issued from the assembly. Mabel flushed. A storm of desire, anger, fear, and shame shot her full of adrenaline. As Brick approached the podium, she threw her hands up and blurted "What the hell are you doing here?" raising her eyebrows and her voice.

"I have a contract!" Brick exclaimed, offering her the heavy bundle. He looked utterly confident, but there was a note of lovesick desperation in his voice. That was not lost on Mabel nor the crowd of union members who sat gawking.

Brick turned to address the crowd. "The board has agreed to 90% of your proposal!" he cried out. More gasps erupted from the members. Andrea and Chris exchanged looks but said nothing, simply stunned.

Mabel snatched the contract, her mouth still agape. She narrowed her eyes and carefully began to flip through it, page by page, scanning each section for the key points. The union members were on the edges of their metal folding chairs, sweating, leaning forward in silent hope that this was no stunt. Mabel was aware of the tension and suspense around her, but she wasn't about to rush her assessment. After a few minutes, breathless silence gave way to curious whispers and speculations. She ignored it all and kept moving through the document, intensely focused, breathing hard.

Brick stood there all the while, watching Mabel reading the contract. At first, her eyes were wide with incredulity, but as she read, little by little, they relaxed, then brightened. Next, her jaw relaxed, and the corners of her mouth began to curl into a smile.

"We won!" she suddenly exclaimed, looking up from the stack, puncturing the sea of murmurs with her voice, like a bugle sounding. "We won! This is it!" She was breathless, and then a wild grin broke across her face like sunlight through the forest canopy. She jumped up and down and held the contract up high. Brick grinned, feeling vicarious joy for her and for everyone in this room. He couldn't take his eyes off of her, she was so beautiful in this moment, her moment of triumph.

She was caught up in a kind of ecstasy, and he wanted to be inside this whirling storm of happy emotion with her. He wanted to hug her or at least get a high five, but he was still conscious of the awkward position they were in. He knew he should step away, but he simply could not remove himself from her radiance.

A cheer roared through the room, and hundreds of arms were thrown up, fists in the air, in the universal gesture of victory. People got up out of their seats, and they hugged each other, crying, some doing little dances, some jumping up and down, some pulling out their phones to share the good news. Mabel had been looking around at the crowd, but now she stopped jumping, hugged the contract, and stood still, smiling at Brick. He returned her smile, asking her a question with his eyes. She knew what she wanted to say, but was too self-conscious, too exposed here. Just then, Andrea walked up and touched Mabel on the shoulder.

"You did it!" she praised. Mabel hugged Andrea and felt endorphins flooding her body, a physical manifestation of the relief she felt, her muscles relaxing into the hug.

"*We* did it," Mabel corrected, gesturing back and forth between herself and Brick.

Andrea turned to him and reached out her hand. "Mr. Feld, I want to say thank you. I don't know how you did it, but thank you."

Brick turned toward Andrea, shook her hand heartily, and shook his head in protest. "Mabel's tireless advocacy and absolutely impeccable attention to detail won this contract for you. I was only the messenger."

"I know Mabel is a formidable negotiator. But I must say, I'm surprised you convinced Mr. Lowe to accept our proposal. I expected at least a week of the strike before he would even begin to budge."

"Actually, he didn't budge at all, but I went to the board, and they were more receptive."

Andrea nodded. "Wow. That took a lot of guts, going over your boss' head."

"It was the only way possible."

"Well, thank you for that advocacy," Andrea lauded and turned to Mabel. "I'm going to call that reporter and give her the update, and then

I'll write up the official communique to the membership. Congratulations again, Mabel. Great work!"

"Thanks, Andrea."

Now, they were standing alone together again, surrounded by *hundreds* of people.

Brick was wringing his hands. "I need to talk to you, Mabel. Can we go somewhere and just talk?" His eyes implored her.

Mabel's breath caught in her chest. "I...yes, I want to talk to you, but we definitely have to get away from here. We still can't be seen together, Brick." She looked around furtively and noticed most people were engaged in their own conversations. A few rows back and to the left, she noticed the member with the big hair, the one who had accused her earlier, staring at them with a look of steep disapproval. She smiled and waved at the woman, then turned back to Brick, trying to look nonchalant. "There's still a lot of heat around all this." She gestured with her index finger, back and forth between herself and Brick.

"Yeah, for sure..." Brick was feeling hotter by the second, but he worked hard to contain it. "Do you want to come to my place?"

"Okay. Just text me your address. But not here. You should leave first, in a few minutes, and I'll stay another twenty minutes or so. Just go talk to some other union members first. We need to make it seem natural."

"Got it." He nodded, then walked away without a wave or a goodbye and waded out into the crowd.

Brick heard the doorbell and rushed to shove a few more random items into the closet. He looked around and sighed—it was the best he could do on short notice. He hoped Mabel wouldn't judge him too harshly. He'd already taken off his suit jacket, and now he removed his tie and threw it onto the coffee table. He opened the door, and there she was, looking both mysterious and radiant in the low light emitted by the elegant wall sconces in the hallway. She had her hands behind her back and was clearly hiding something there.

"Hi, Mabel. Please, come in..." he stepped back, and she walked over the threshold, entering his living room/dining room.

"Shoes off?" Mabel asked. She had noticed a small shoe rack just inside the door.

"Yes, thank you," Brick replied, nodding. Mabel slipped off her strappy heels and looked around. She noticed several bookshelves stuffed full, displaying the colorful spines of books of all different heights and widths. He had a beautiful array of oversized house plants crowded near the large window at the far end of the room. There was no TV, but she saw his laptop sitting slightly askew on the end table near the couch. She turned to face Brick and pulled a bottle of champagne from a bag she had been holding behind her back.

"For you!" she sang, holding it forth.

"Oh, thank you..." Brick voiced, taking it and reading the label.

"Thank *you* for sticking your neck out for us, Brick. You really surprised me."

"I told you I could surprise you, Mabel...let me get a few glasses, and we can celebrate our success. Go ahead and have a seat," he gestured in the direction of the couch, "Please, make yourself at home."

Mabel nodded, walked over to the soft, sky-blue sofa, and sat down. She messed with her hair and poked around his coffee table. There was a Rubix cube, unsolved, an empty but lightly used coffee mug, Brick's tie, the one he'd been wearing earlier in the evening, some mail, and several magazines stacked up. Under those, she could see *the paper*, the one with their kiss engulfing the front page. She picked it up, and the memory of his mouth rushed back for the billionth time. She heard Brick coming back and stuffed the paper under the magazines again, sitting up straight, trying to calm her heartbeat.

Brick sauntered in looking casual, carrying two wine glasses full of bubbly, and sat down closer than she had expected him to. He offered her a glass, and she accepted with a smile.

"Cheers!" they proclaimed in unison, and then they laughed, clinked their glasses, and each took a sip. There was a moment of silence where they just looked at each other, and it wasn't really awkward, just intense.

It was Mabel who finally broke the silence. "So how did you really do this, Brick? It doesn't make any sense. After that horrible meeting with Marshall, I was sure we were in a deadlock."

"You didn't open my letter..." Brick raised one eyebrow at her.

She winced. "Yeah...no...I was going to, but...well, I didn't trust myself with you...with all this going on...I was planning to open it after all this blew over. I'm sorry, I just couldn't..."

"No, I get it. You were in a tough spot..."

"That photo! Oh my god...you don't know how mortified I've been this week..."

"I know...my God, me too. We didn't even get to talk about all that, the fallout..."

"The fallout! It really fucked me up. I let the union down." She shook her head. "They had a right to be mad, but I mean, those people were ready to tear my limbs off tonight! It looked so bad...no one believed me that we weren't..." She tilted her head with the suggestion of what they weren't but could have been doing...

"I'm really sorry. I feel like it was my fault..."

"No, it wasn't your fault. It was hot, and..." Mabel took another sip of the champagne to give herself courage.

"And what?"

"And I was vibing on you," Mabel admitted, nodding her head and giving him a sly smile.

"I was vibing on you. I like you *a lot,* Mabel." He leaned in a little, and Mabel felt her legs turn to mush.

"Is that what you wrote in the letter?" she asked, raising her eyebrows.

"Not exactly...I mean, in an indirect way, yes. But actually, the envelope held a copy of my letter of resignation."

"*What?*"

"Yeah, I sent that letter to the board on Friday. I decided I couldn't work for this company any more, not with Lowe in charge. He's such an ignorant asshole...and anyway–"

"That's...wow...but then why did you come today? And why did they sign the contract?"

63

"They read the letter, and they called me in, and we had a very long, very honest conversation, and I was able to make them see the benefits of signing your contract, and, well, basically, they offered me CEO."

"Are you *serious?*" Mabel gawked at Brick for the second time that night.

"Yes. They fired Lowe!"

"Oh wow." Mabel went silent, thinking about the implications of this. She felt a weird sinking feeling on one hand and relief on the other. This was great for the *workers* to have an ally in that position, but personally.... "So...did you accept the job?" she asked, nervous energy inflecting the tone of her voice.

"Not yet. I...I wanted to talk to you first." Brick set down his champagne glass on the coffee table.

"Me? About what?" she asked, setting her own glass down.

"About you. About *us*. I don't want to work for this company if it means I can't get close to you, Mabel."

Mabel felt her face flush, and her whole body go warm and electric.

"I want to be close to you," she reflected. "I don't want to fight it anymore. I want to give in."

He leaned toward her and she pounced like a lioness, pushing him down on the couch. She was very strong, and although he was stronger and could have easily resisted this motion, he liked the force of her body and the power of her will, so he let her pin him down. He liked to feel the weight of her, the draping of her body over his. He could feel her breasts against his chest as she pressed her mouth to his, and he tasted her again. He closed his eyes, welcoming her tongue, sucking and biting on her lips like a hungry animal.

Mabel lost herself in the kiss—releasing a tension wound up so tight it frightened her, the intensity of her desire coursing through her bloodstream and heating up every muscle in her body, making her skin hot to the touch. Until this moment, she hadn't realized just how much she desired him.

Meanwhile, Brick was so thirsty he couldn't absorb all the sensations fast enough. He ran his hands down her back and along the ample curve of her ass, gripping her and pulling her tighter against him. She moaned into his mouth. He pulled away and whispered into her ear, "Tell me what you want, Mabel."

"I want your mouth on me everywhere," she confessed.

"Mmmm. I want to taste every square inch of you..." he expressed, and kissed her neck and sucked on the soft skin of her throat. She moaned again.

Mabel felt her pussy come alive, glistening wet. "I want *all* of you," she purred, moving her fingers over his shoulders and down his highly defined biceps. There was too much fabric between her hands and his skin. She started to unbutton his shirt from the neck down. He released her neck from his mouth, pushed her up again, and pulled himself up, facing her, so he could give her access to the lower buttons and get his hands up under her shirt. He felt her up slowly, feeling her nipples against the palms of his hands and gently kneading the flesh, exploring the gauzy fabric that hugged her curves. It wasn't enough to touch. He needed to see her body. He kissed her again, then lifted her red blouse over her head and feasted his eyes upon her breasts, gasping at how sexy she looked in her red lace underwire bra. *Just like her to color coordinate even her underclothes,* he thought.

Now Mabel pulled his shirt off of his shoulders and ran her hands over his chest, smiling mischievously at him. He pulled the straps of her bra down and kissed each of her shoulders. She peeled his shirt down his arms and freed his hands, which he promptly used to reach behind her back and unclasp her bra. Her breasts popped free of constraint, and he yanked her bra all the way off, admiring the large circles of her areolas topped with pert, hard nipples.

"Lie down. I want to undress you," Brick demanded.

Mabel took down her hair first, shaking it out, and looked at him with a bonfire in her eyes. Then she laid back and pulled her feet up onto the couch, knees bent, legs spread, inviting him into her most personal space. Brick ran his hands down her thighs and stroked her over her pants. She gasped, and he moved to unbutton and unzip her dress slacks, revealing the matching red lace underwear he expected to see. He yanked her pants over the curves of her hips but left the panties on, for now. He freed her legs and relished the smooth skin of her calves and the muscular curves of her thighs. He could see she was a serious rock climber. With one hand on her thigh, he used the fingertips of his other hand to stroke Mabel's mound over the lace. Her body shuddered, and she made a swooning sound. He could see and feel her neatly groomed hair, a thin strip above the opening, and further down, he felt her moisture, warm and fragrant.

Brick was quite aware of his dick fighting to get out of his pants, but he wanted to linger here and give Mabel what she had asked for. He climbed over her and kissed her mouth again, this time slowly and deeply. She wrapped her arms around his back and pulled him down on top of her until she could feel his bare chest against hers and the pressure, through his pants, of his hard cock against her warm center. He rubbed against her, and she curled her legs around his hips, encouraging the grind. She sucked on his lower lip, moving her hands up to hold his face. He kissed her right hand and proceeded to kiss all the way down her arm to her shoulder, her collarbone, and up the other arm. Mabel smiled at his attention to detail, eagerly awaiting the movement of his mouth down, down, down her chest, her belly, her–.

He soon obliged, inching his mouth into the space between her breasts and moving along the right side, hungrily licking and sucking the flesh. Her chest was rising and falling erratically now, quicker and quicker, the closer he got to the nipple. He licked all around it on the one side, fondling the other side with his hand, and finally licked the tip. Her hands were in his hair now, and she cried out. He sucked and nibbled on her for some time, then switched to the other side, enjoying the sounds of pleasure from Mabel, her voice growing to a low growl, her arousal blossoming.

Keeping his hands firmly on her breasts, he inched his mouth down her belly, kissing her lovely innie. Then he kissed lower and lower until he met the delicate texture of the red lace. Then he slid his hands down to meet the leading edge of his desire. He slipped his fingers up under the fabric and gently explored the wet folds, discovering her fully swollen clit, which he circled a few times, teasing her, before tracing the opening itself. She was writhing under his touch now. He pulled the panties off, *finally*, and used his tongue, tracing the path his fingers had traveled moments before, and tasted her juices. Now she was wet like summer rain and moaning and cooing in response to his warm mouth searching her most delicate flesh, causing tremors that foreshadowed something cataclysmic.

"I want to feel you, deep..." Mabel said longingly.

"You'll have to wait a little longer.." Brick murmured, coming up for air. "I need to work your beautiful legs.."

Mabel was desperate for his cock but appreciated the slow, seductive kisses down the inner surface of each thigh. Her pussy was vibrating now, and each brush of his lips was such sweet torture. He lifted one leg and kissed her behind her knee, then along the muscular curve of her calf, like he was tracing an old-fashioned stocking seam down the back of her leg, all the way to her foot. He kissed the top side of her foot and each of her toes. After that, he looked up at her and raised an eyebrow. She beckoned him with her index finger. He stood up from the couch and slowly unbuckled his belt, unzipped his pants, and let them fall to the ground. Mabel watched him in suspense. Now she could see his cock pressing against his black boxer briefs. He peeled them off and let it out, and it was long and rigid, standing straight up, made of stone, but with a soft tip and a clear droplet of his desire poised at the precipice. Mabel longed to lick it off and taste him but thought better of it. She was not one to let her lust overcome her health and safety. She didn't know Brick all that well, let's be honest.

"We need a condom," she declared soberly but also with a tone of urgent need.

"I've got it covered," Brick assured, reaching for the drawer in his coffee table. "No pun intended," he joked, holding up the condom.

Mabel giggled. "Were you planning on this, or do you just regularly seduce women on your couch?"

"Neither. I like to be *prepared,* that's all," he said, a sparkle in his eye.

Mabel smirked, took it from his hand, and tore it open, tossing the package on the coffee table. Then she dressed him deftly. He gasped at her touch, her slender fingers rolling the rubber down the length of his cock.

"Come on then, boy scout.." she teased. "There might be a merit badge at the end of this, depending on how you perform." Mabel raised one eyebrow. Brick climbed over her, aimed, and hit the target, pushing into her slowly but firmly as he looked into her eyes. Her beautiful brown eyes went wide, and she moaned. Brick kissed her mid-moan and began moving his hips, going slowly, savoring the sensation of her warmth surrounding him. Her mouth felt just as warm, her tongue teasing him. He sucked on her lips, thrusting a little faster and a little harder, feeling her body opening to him. He pulled away from her mouth and bit her neck, pushing a little deeper, feeling his cock light up, practically glowing. He was so fucking aroused.

"Yes!" she crooned. "Oh my God, you feel so good..."

"I've wanted you so badly, Mabel," Brick whispered into her ear. He was starting to sweat a little now, his breath quickening. "It was so hard to stop wanting you."

"Don't stop!" Mabel pleaded, wrapping her arms around his back, digging into his skin with her flawless French manicure. The pressure of her nails excited him, and he moved in her faster still, the friction building toward the edge of ecstasy. With each thrust, Mabel grew more excited, and she vocalized her pleasure, to his great delight. The sound of her voice was driving him crazy with lust.

Brick was all pent up over her and knew he could go at any moment, but at the same time, he was enjoying her so much, and she clearly wanted more, so he slowed the pace just a little. He pushed himself up onto his arms so he could look down at her beautiful body, her gorgeous brown skin glistening with a mixture of both their sweats now. Mabel reached up and put her hands on either side of his face. He turned his head just enough to kiss her left hand.

She drew her index finger across his lips. He licked her finger and started sucking on it. She gasped and felt a tingle run down her spine all the way to her toes. Keeping one hand posted to hold him up, he kept fucking her and sucking her fingers and used his other hand on her nipples, stroking and squeezing them. Mabel started to whimper. She moved her hand along his mouth, imagining his tongue on her clit. He sucked on each of her fingers in turn, all the while continuing to light up her tits with his touch, now pinching, now circling the areola, now brushing the tip lightly, a sweet torture. When he had sucked all the way down to her pinky, she took her hand away from his mouth and moved it down her stomach slowly, meeting the place where Brick was entering her. She touched his cock, letting her fingers graze it, feeling her own wetness coating it. She then stroked his abs, which were working hard at that moment. Soon she began to stroke her clit, her voice trembling, and this drove Brick wild. Seeing her touching herself made him slow down again, teasing her, pulling out of her slowly and thrusting hard, fast, and deep. His fingers still fondled her breasts, and he leaned down and started nibbling on her ear.

"Yes!" she pleaded, and he felt her fingers moving faster down below and he followed her into a feverish, pounding rhythm. Mabel was overwhelmed by the symphony of sensations, and she let go, closed her eyes, and lost all awareness of the world outside of her body. The thrumming, the jolt of full-body pleasure took her breath away, and then she gasped for air and cried out, and he felt her pussy squeezing him, pulsating, and it sent him into his own spiral, and he pushed harder and faster, coming deep inside her still-vibrating pussy, calling her name. When he was spent, he collapsed on top of her.

"Wow...that was something," Brick choked out, still panting.

"I'm saying! I confess I've been guessing you'd be good in bed."

"Really? You've been thinking about me, huh?"

"Yes, and I was not disappointed."

"So, I earned the merit badge?" he asked, raising an eyebrow.

"One hundred percent. You really got me off–that was an uncommonly deep and powerful orgasm."

Brick laughed. "You made it easy. You're so sexy!" He kissed her deeply

"Thank you," Mabel beamed. "Look who's talking." She stroked his chest seductively.

"Just a second," Brick said, "I've got to be thorough." He pulled out of her and dealt with the condom.

"Thank you for that."

"Thank *you! So,* well, next, I need to learn to climb. Will you be my teacher?"

Mabel smirked. "That would be a lot of fun. All this feels so right to me, Brick, but outside your apartment, we still have all that drama, the jobs...What are we going to do?"

"I don't know. We'll figure it out. No turning back, Mabel. No one else will do for me. I've got to be with you."

"I want to be with you and follow this thread we've got going. But I'm not leaving the union."

"I know. I wouldn't want that. It's time for me to make a change."

"But Brick, how can you turn down being CEO? What about your family? How will you support them?"

"I'll figure it out. We'll figure it out."

Chapter Eleven

Mabel's phone went off. It was her friend, Lelia, from college–calling from way out in North Dakota.

"Oh my God, Lelia! How are you?" she gasped.

"Mabel, I'm glad you're still up. I hope I'm not interrupting you, but I'm so angry I could spit fire."

Mabel could hear the fire in her friend's voice, and now she was very concerned! "No, girl, you can call me at any hour!" she insisted. "What happened? I haven't talked to you in so long!"

"My annoying boss is what happened! I quit my job this evening. He is such an asshole."

"Is this the same boss who hired you six months ago?"

"Yup."

"I thought you said he was a *hottie*? I remember you were so excited to work with him! What did he do?"

"He is a hot *asshole*. Everything was fine, and then today, in a staff meeting, he dressed me down, calling me an incompetent assistant. The others latched on, and for the rest of the day, I had to deal with snide remarks and disrespect."

"Oh no he did *not!* Did you file a complaint with HR? He can't get away with treating you that way, Lelia." Mabel fumed. She knew her friend to be highly intelligent, hardworking, and organized. "You shouldn't have to quit. They need to fix this. Or if they won't, they need to pay you out. It sounds like workplace discrimination. You need me to come out there? I *will* talk to your HR department."

"He's not worth going to war with HR over. However, by quitting, I'm leaving him in a lurch. Next week, he has a meeting with Hendrick Pfieffer, Chaundra's boss, and I have all the research. So let's see how he does without me!"

"Ooo, girl, you are dodging a bullet there, too. Hendrick is *crazy*! Maybe it's good your boss is an asshole because when you mess with Hendrick...you never know what's gonna transpire. You know about Chaundra's 'team building' exercises?"

"Hendrick Pfieffer wants to be Loki, the god of mischief and Cupid combined the way he decides to meddle in people's lives. Hence, Chaundra and her office mates. By the way, how are negotiations going for your new contract? Were you able to get that hard ass, what's his name, to work things out?"

"Brick? Well...you could say so...Yes, we got the contract! And this is crazy, but I think I'm in love with that hard ass...we are *dating!*"

"Say what now?"

Mabel could hear that Lelia's eyes were popping out of her head. "I got him to see we needed the contract, and he made it happen, and then we realized we really liked each other..."

"That's my girl. You not only negotiated a new contract but one for your personal life. I need to take lessons from you! I think I'm getting tired of coming home to an empty condo."

"Girl, I know that feeling. I was in a very long and very dry spell before *all this* happened."

"At least tell me you are happy with the relationship and that it won't become an HR problem for the two of you."

"I'm so happy, Lelia, I feel like I could explode! I was worried about HR, but we got the company to approve our relationship. Brick is taking over the CEO position for the next year, so I'm not really working with him directly. Anyway, there are no negotiations for the next year, so there isn't a conflict of interest. We just had to sign some disclosure papers."

"He's the CEO? I thought way back when you said you would never date a corporate man. I also remember you saying that they don't understand the worker bees and look down on them. What's changed? Don't think I'm not happy for you, but what made you flip the switch?"

"He's different, Lelia. He's not your typical annoying boss. I found a unicorn, I swear to God. We have all these ideas for how to make the company more *responsive* to the worker bees! I literally don't know if he'll last, though, because he might be too much on our side."

"If they don't fire him, I think you and he would make a great partnership fighting for the rights of the workers."

"True that. Whatever happens, I feel like we will thrive. It feels like this is the real thing, Lelia. He told me he loved me for the first time this week, and I believe him!"

"This dude sounds like he's got game."

"I'ma send you a picture right now..." Mabel quickly texted Lelia a pic of Brick in his new rock climbing gear she just bought him for his birthday.

"He's a cutie! Have you guys gotten busy yet? Wait a minute, tell me there was at least a first date."

"We hooked up spontaneously the night we got the contract–"

"Oh my God..."

"It was so scandalous and so delicious! Our first real date didn't happen till a few weeks later, because we couldn't be seen out in public, but it was so romantic...we went for dinner at the top of the WCP building, that really fancy place with the exotic cocktails. And we watched the sunset. Then we went to the hot springs outside of town...girl, mmmm..."

"I'm so glad this works for you. If anyone deserves love and happiness, it's you, so hold on with both hands and enjoy the ride."

"Thanks, Lelia. You deserve the same! I know yours is coming. I'm so glad you are getting out of that toxic work environment!"

"Speaking of toxic work environments, that annoying asshole was blowing my phone up the whole time we were talking. Look, girl, my dinner is almost done, so I'm going to grab a bottle of wine and get settled. Oh, that's right, Davida is coming over and bringing bubbly. Call me anytime with updates. I love that you are in love."

"I love you, Lelia! I'm so glad you called! Have a great night! Fuck the boss! Let's get all the girls on video call soon because it's been too long–I don't care how busy we are. We need to make time. This is restorative."

"I know, right? We do need a video call to catch up. I honestly have missed you, ladies!"

"Same! I will tell Chaundra, you call Crystal."

"Got it! Love you!"

"Love you!"

Epilogue

SATURDAY...NINE MONTHS AFTER THAT

"Ok, reach up to that craggy bit above your head and put your right foot in the crevice a little above your right knee..."

Brick looked up, then down to his knee. "Oh, of course. Okay...got it..."

Mabel watched him attack the hold. His biceps bulged, then he moved his foot and hefted himself up another few feet before stopping to study his next move. She kept quiet now, enjoying her view of his ass in the harness. She didn't like to direct him unless he was really stuck. Like all new climbers, he would have to learn for himself the pain of burning out your arms too quickly, trying to pull up on everything.

"Don't forget to clip in up there." Mabel reminded him. Brick was fearless, which was a good thing, but he suffered a little bit from male overconfidence, and he liked to show off in her presence. She had to keep reminding him that savvy climbing required caution and that she was most impressed when he demonstrated a slow and thoughtful climb.

After a few seconds, he was on the move again. She watched him with admiration—all-in-all, he was a good student and was making a lot of progress. She let him get about thirty feet ahead of her, then followed him, moving like Spiderman up the cliff. When he reached the top, she could tell because she heard him whoop his triumph, his voice echoing across the canyon. Then he stood and peered over the edge, watching his girlfriend expertly choose holds with the strength and grace of a dancer.

"Show-off!" he teased. "You always tell me to take it slow, then you do *that*!"

Mabel looked up and grinned. "It's not the same thing! I've climbed this one a *million times*. Don't worry, you'll get there!" She winked at him, then continued climbing and quickly reached the top, pulling herself up easily. She was dewy from sweat, and her face was radiant. Brick took in the look of her in that cropped tank top and cargo shorts and almost swooned. *How was he so lucky?*

"Nice work! You did that really well, for a *noob*." Mabel put her hand up for a high five.

"Thank you. I have the most *skilled* instructor..." he confided, and with this, he pulled her to him, wrapped his arms around her, and kissed her deeply. Then they stood side by side, admiring the view of the gorge, the river rushing far below. Mabel pulled an energy bar out of her pack, opened it, broke it evenly in two, and gave half to Brick.

"Mmmm, thank you. I love the peanut butter flavor!"

"I know, that's why I packed it."

"I love you."

"I know..." she smirked, pulling her phone from her pocket. She was wearing men's climbing shorts, more tomboy than her usual style, and a little oversized because, apparently, the niche clothing companies designing outerwear for climbers didn't think women needed pockets. Brick thought she looked sexy in them, men's shorts or not.

"Let's commemorate our one-year anniversary," she announced. She handed her phone to Brick, and he framed their flushed faces with the mountains in the background. This was protocol since his arms were longer and better suited to capture a wide-angle selfie. Smiling into the camera, she recalled the day they first hooked up. What a year! Brick handed back the phone, and she quickly navigated the menus to add this last pic to the slideshow.

"I made something for you, Brick...a surprise."

"Oh?" Brick replied, raising his eyebrows, intrigued.

"Let's sit on the ledge," Mabel gestured. When they were comfortably seated, legs hanging over the rock face, she held her phone so he could see, and she pressed play on the slideshow. It began with the notorious front page photo of their indiscretion at the park a year ago to the day. Brick gasped, and Mabel giggled.

"The first picture of us together, *ever*," he reminisced, "and it almost *ruined* us!"

"I know, right? Most people don't have a picture of their first kiss. Actually, almost *no one* does...we're kind of freaky!"

"*Kind of?*...Our first date...I remember that light on your face at sunset that night..."

"Our first county fair, which was also our first Ferris wheel ride together..."

"You had to *prove* to me you weren't afraid of heights..."

"Labor Day barbecue at Rodney's, so: first time hanging out with all our mutual friends as a *couple,* but the second time in the *pool* together...damn you look hot in a bikini, Mabel!" Brick gaped, putting his hand on her thigh.

"Thank you! I blame *all of this* on that bikini..."

"First Thanksgiving with your family...that was a *fantastic* meal. Okay, I'm picking up on a theme here..."

"Oh, our first double date with Chaundra and Casey! Remember how they kept teasing us?"

"Yes, as if *they* weren't a scandalous pair and just as disgustingly cute! Ugh, even *more* disgusting, in my opinion..."

"First snowy day together!" In the photo, they were bundled up in huge coats with fur-lined hoods. Mabel's hood was down and snowflakes were scattered here and there throughout her hair.

"Remember our night in that cabin with the fireplace...?"

"Mmmm, baby, I loved having you there on that fluffy rug by the fire..."

"First night at karaoke!"

"The night I found out you can *really* sing..."

"Our first trip to the Jersey shore...oo my calf looks *angry*..."

Mabel cracked up. "I remember how incensed you were that a jellyfish took the trouble to sting you."

"I was innocent!"

"Oh, you like to *play* innocent..."

"First time we took Roswell on a long hike..."

Pictures kept flowing—selfies all around town, up in New York City at their first Broadway play.

The slideshow ended, and Brick kissed Mabel slowly. She took his face in her hands and they both dissolved into each other.

"So many firsts for us, Mabel..." Brick announced when they finally came up for air.

"It's hard to believe a year has gone by..." she remarked.

"I know...it feels like it went fast in one way, but on the other hand, so much has happened for us, personally and professionally..."

"Hey, how are you feeling about leaving the company? I can't believe this is your last week..."

"It's a mix, you know? It's been a good year, and I finally feel proud of what I do."

"Crestline Industries has changed so much, Brick. It's almost unrecognizable!"

"Yeah, a year ago, I couldn't have imagined the labor summit or the *listening sessions* with management or the union electing a special board member to be the voice of the workers. "

"Yessica is going to *kill* it on the board."

"I have no doubt," Brick agreed, nodding his head.

"It's like your *baby* at this point. I kind of hate to see you leave it, Brick," Mabel lamented. "I don't like that our relationship is forcing you to leave."

"It's your baby, *too,* Mabel. We worked together on this. I know you'll hold it down and keep the new CEO accountable to the workers."

"Oh, you *know* I will," Mabel affirmed.

"But also, I'm ready for a change, and you are *so* much more important to me than any job could ever be."

"I love you, Brick."

"I love you more!" Brick countered. Mabel took his face in her hands, and they kissed, a long, slow kiss that made Brick want to ravish her right there, at the park. When she finally pulled away, he took her hands in his.

"I also have a surprise for *you*!" he exclaimed.

"Oo! I love surprises! What is it?"

"I planned a trip for us to California in a few weeks..."

"What?" Mabel gawked, her eyes all lit up. "Where? When?"

"We'll leave September 10th and stay for two weeks."

"Two weeks?!"

"Well, I'm free for a bit while I job search, and this is the most beautiful time of year in the Bay Area..."

"I don't know if I can get time *off* though..." Mabel agonized. "The new contract negotiations are starting soon..."

"I already checked in with Andrea to make sure it was okay for you to be away right now. She gave us her blessing. They won't start negotiations without you."

"What?! You two conspired? You really are a *little* cozy with the union, Mr. Feld." Mabel admonished, hitting him lightly on the arm.

"See, that's just another reason I need to *quit*..." Brick shrugged, smiling.

"Eek! I'm so excited! I haven't had a real vacation in such a long time!"

"You've been busy. You've really *earned* it, Mabel."

"I'm ready! I need a *breather*."

"I've prepared an itinerary for us..." Brick pulled out a folded piece of paper from his back pocket and handed it to Mabel. "I want to take you to see the giant redwoods. I want to take you climbing in Yosemite and to the ocean, and you'll get to meet my family and friends...I thought you'd be interested in the Rosie the Riveter Museum in Richmond..."

She unfolded it and eagerly read the list of stops and excursions, all mapped out. Brick and she were both planners, and she appreciated that. "This looks amazing, Brick! Thank you!"

"I'm open to adding to it or changing if you have other things you'd like to see or do. This is all for you, Mabel. The only thing that's locked in is the camping reservation—it's a *miracle* I got that spot. Usually, you have to reserve six months in advance..."

"I'll think about it and do some research, but I trust you know all the best places."

"It is my *home*—or was my home. It was my *first* home. You are my new home, Mabel." Brick cooed, putting his arms around her and gazing into her eyes.

"I'm so glad you feel that way. You know, I've been thinking maybe it's time we actually share a physical home..."

"Interesting..."

* * *

Sunday, three months after that

"Hey man, thanks for coming over." Brick hugged Rodney as he came in the door, carrying a six-pack of beer and a couple of hoagies. The living room was a veritable obstacle course, with different sized moving boxes all over the place, all at various stages of being packed with Brick's belongings.

"Of course!" Rodney said, picking his way across the space to set the lunch down on Brick's dining room table. "Moving is a lot."

"At least I'm only moving across town and not across the country this time."

"You ready for this? Cohabitation?" Rodney queried, raising his eyebrows with a smile.

Brick shook his head. "I've never lived with a girlfriend before. I'm stepping out on a ledge, Rodney. It's thrilling and *terrifying*. That's how pretty much everything has been since Mabel came into my life."

"Love will do that to you."

"I guess so."

"To be real, I knew this day was coming. I didn't want to spook you, so I didn't say anything, not to you or to Mabel, but...I could see it was serious the first time I saw you two out in public together, officially, as a couple."

"What, at the county fair?"

"Yeah, I've known Mabel practically her whole life, and she is a passionate person, ok, but I've never seen her so lit up. She was straight doting on you, feeding you funnel cake..."

"Oh right, that was my first funnel cake!"

"Plus the way she roasts you..." Rodney smiled and shook his head. "That is a show of *deep* affection."

Brick laughed. "Ya I can feel that. I think I was never truly in love before—I think I *thought* I was, but all that was immature, and I didn't know myself. I think my other relationships only scratched the surface. This shit is *deep*."

"It's beautiful what you two have created. I'm really happy for you both."

"Thanks, Rodney. What about you? Have you been in love?"

"Yeah, a few times. And I've been *out* of love. Still looking for the one..."

"How's the dating game?"

"Meh. This town is too small."

"You on the apps?"

"Nah. Man, I don't like the apps."

"I get it. Well, I know someone is coming down the pipeline, one way or another."

"We'll see."

Acknowledgments

This novel has been a true labor of love, supported by the love of so many people in my life. I want to thank my family for giving me time, space and encouragement to complete this project. I want to give a huge shout out to the Sunday Romance Writers' group, without whose camaraderie, sense of humor and inspiration, I could not have succeeded. Special thanks to my inner writer circle, Ruby D. Flowers, Octavia Price and Lynette Angelica Sivad for all your extra words of encouragement and gentle prodding. Much gratitude to the many Romance industry authors and professionals who lent their time and expertise to the Sunday Romance Writers: Eva O'Hare, Pepper Pace, Reana Malori, Jailaa West, Carla Truss, Reana Malori, Joe Federico and Harper Black. Finally, many thanks to Tori Moore, a most fabulous editor, who offered expert feedback that has helped me improve my craft and bring this story to life, and to press.

About The Author

Eliza has always been a romantic! She started chasing boys around the yard in first grade and never stopped, right up until the day her soul mate and co-pilot dropped into her lap in her early twenties. Eliza has long dreamed of being a writer, and has dabbled in poetry and fiction over the years, with many stops and starts. This is her first novel and she is delighted to share it with you! In her spare time, Eliza loves to read, play music, craft, and spend time in the great outdoors with her husband and her daughter.

www.ingramcontent.com/pod-product-compliance
Lightning Source LLC
Chambersburg PA
CBHW020547130626
46552CB00007B/2798